Doubly Departed

An Amanda Winters Mystery

by

Carmen Will

Copyright 2016 by Carmen Will

For information, email **Cozy Cat Press**, cozycatpress@aol.com or visit our website at: www.cozycatpress.com

COZY CAT
PRESS

ISBN: 978-1-946063-00-7

Printed in the United States of America

Cover design by Paula Ellenberger
www.paulaellenberger.com

1 2 3 4 5 6 7 8 9 10

Dedication

To Wayne, who has never—not for a moment—stopped pushing, prodding, and praying…I love you!

Prologue
Friday

Pedaling along Mill Avenue in downtown Tempe, Nathan Reynolds dodged between groups of high-spirited students determined to make the most of their winter break. He knew that his friends would be trying to pack in as much partying as possible before classes resumed on Monday, but Nathan would not be participating in the night's festivities. He promised Danielle that he'd catch up with her later for a movie—but first he had some business to take care of.

Nearly ten years after his dad had left without so much as a good-bye, Nathan was on his way to meet someone who finally might be able to give him some answers. For years, Nathan had been scouring the Internet each day, Googling his dad's name and hoping that something would turn up. But nothing ever did. Nathan knew his dad wasn't the kind who'd give his kid a Zebco Rhino Spincast rod for his eleventh birthday, promise him a weekend trip to Apache Lake to break it in, and then just take off without even a good-bye.

Nathan pedaled harder and faster along Mill Avenue. The crowds were beginning to thin as students staked out places at their favorite bars, already buzzing with activity. Just inside the open doors of a popular Tempe hangout, a band was playing, its music lively and loud, the amped-up bass of a guitar powerful enough to pound in his chest as he rode past. He spotted a group of Danielle's friends and waved, but they didn't see him. They were too busy making idiots of themselves, throwing back shots and trying to impress the guys in the band.

At Tempe Beach Park, Nathan turned right onto Rio Salado Parkway. He pulled his bike off the pedestrian path in front of the Art Center and gazed out at the lake. The damp chill in the air started to make his eyes water, and he drew the hood of his jacket more tightly around his face.

"Nathan?"

"Yeah...hi." He hadn't heard the man approach. Because he'd been caught off-guard, his voice had cracked as if it belonged to some dopey kid on the verge of puberty.

Nathan studied the strange figure amid a gray dusk that was rapidly sinking into darkness. There was something off about the guy. His appearance didn't jibe with his voice, a deep, confident voice that sounded like it belonged to someone important. The man had a scraggly beard and long black hair topped with a red bandanna, and he wore a dirty gray sweatshirt that had some sort of gross stain on the front. Nathan took comfort in the fact that he'd ignored the man's request that he bring along his dad's box—the one he'd found in his mom's garage last week—and instead hid it where no one would find it for a while.

The man smiled, and the two exchanged a firm handshake. "I thought the Keg would be a good place to grab some dinner." Nathan followed his gaze upward and saw shallow tiers of dark clouds scudding in from the mountains.

"Looks like rain," the man said. He pointed toward a black pickup parked at the edge of the lot adjacent to the Salt River's south bank. "We can put your bike in the back of my truck, and you can stow your laptop under the front seat." He cocked his head. "That sound good to you?"

"Sure. I guess..."

They drove east along the parkway past the golf course and pulled into the lot that served Tempe Marketplace. The man chose a parking spot at the outer edge of the lot, away from the restaurants and shops. "Best place to avoid dings," he said with a smile.

Before opening the passenger door, Nathan gave the man a sidelong glance. Though he was anxious to get some answers, he decided to be patient and hold his questions until they got to the restaurant. They'd started toward the front entrance when the man stopped abruptly to study the area around them. Had he heard something, or seen something in the shadows? The next thing Nathan knew, the muzzle of a gun was digging into his side, and the man was demanding that he hand over his phone.

"We'll be heading over to those trees now, Nathan. And if you make a sound or try anything stupid, I'm going to have to kill you right here."

Nathan shivered. Was the guy a perv? He thought about making a run for it, but the gun dug more deeply into his ribs, as though the man knew what he was thinking. He had no choice but to do as he was told. They walked through a line of towering mesquite trees that separated the parking lot from a dirt path that ran parallel to the river.

The man urged Nathan over a three-foot high barrier. On the other side, a berm that extended the length of the mall overlooked a steep embankment that descended to a dense cover of cottonwoods and pine and, beyond that, the river. The only light that reached them now was a faint glow from the mall above and behind them. As they made their way down the slope, Nathan looked to his right and to his left, hoping to see someone who might be able to help him, but no one else, he realized, would likely be on the rocky downgrade at this hour and risk falling in the darkness. He assumed that they would stop in the midst of the heaviest cover of trees, but the man nudged him clear through the trees to the riverbank.

"But why…" Before Nathan could ask the question, he heard a sharp *pop*. There was a rushing in his ears, and something warm ran down the back of his neck. He was still alive when his body hit the water. His last thought was of his mom, and how very much she would miss him.

Chapter One
Saturday

"Mom! Mom!!"

I struggled to raise myself to an upright position, but my body was dead weight. I fell back onto the floor, where my head hit the tile with a sickening thud.

"Mom!! What happened?!"

My brain tried to respond, but my voice wasn't cooperating. A sound came out of my mouth that was more a croak than a word. "Ye-e-ch."

Something cold and wet was plopped onto my forehead.

"I reached Dad on his cell, and he said to call 9-1-1 if you didn't start to act normal in five minutes."

Normal. Now that would be something.

I rolled to a sitting position again, and this time my body stayed put. A soggy washcloth fell into my lap, and with a grimace I knocked it to the floor. I opened my mouth to speak, and there was no croak this time, only the familiar sound of my son's name. "Jeff."

He retrieved the washcloth from the floor and hoisted it over his shoulder, where it landed with a splash in a sink-full of sudsy water. "Are you okay?"

The room had stopped spinning, light had replaced blackness, and Jeff's handsome face was sharpening into focus.

"I'm fine." I narrowed my eyes and studied him. "Are you growing a beard?"

"Naw. I just didn't feel like shaving this morning."

Secure in the knowledge that his mother would not be dying today, Jeff allowed his body to relax as if the weight of the world had been lifted from his sturdy, 21-year-old shoulders. He reached out to me, and I used his arms to pull myself up. Together, we shuffled over to the kitchen table. He drew out one of the chairs and helped me fall easily into it.

"I'm good now," I said. "Really. It was just a panic attack."

"You scared the crap out of me, Mom. I thought you were dead."

"Sorry. I'm not. Dead, I mean." I felt the back of my head for a lump, and detected the tender beginnings of one. "I guess I must have just passed out for a moment."

Fifteen years earlier, I'd been diagnosed with an assortment of phobias and anxieties the experts have tied up in a neat package termed *Cluster C*. After a significant number of blood tests and scans ruled out physical reasons for my bouts of vertigo, heart palpitations, and the frequent certainty that I was about to take my last breath, I was told I suffered from "acute panic disorder, agoraphobia, and avoidant personality syndrome": Cluster C. There are two options for treatment: antidepressants, which I dislike because of their side effects, and psychotherapy, which I dislike because the whole process is ridiculously expensive and just plain annoying. And so I have decided to live with the evils I know. I have some good days, some bad.

Jeff, not quite convinced that I was "good now," kept a firm hand on my shoulder as he surveyed the kitchen before leveling a reproachful gaze at me. "I told you I was coming to help you unpack today. You should've waited."

"You helped me all day yesterday. Besides, there's still more than enough work around here to keep everyone busy for at least a week."

I studied the room, which did not at all reflect the hours of hard work I was almost sure I'd put in that day. Lining the walls were stacks of boxes, their contents spilling out onto the floor. A row of pots and pans I'd arranged on the counter, their lids askew, seemed to be poised in marching formation, their handles pointed, fascist style, toward us. Plastic trays of flatware and kitchen gadgets covered the faux-wood countertops. A roll of vinyl shelf liner had unfurled across the floor. Had it been red instead of beige stripe, one might have thought I'd rolled out a carpet to welcome William, Kate, and their royal offspring.

Jeff stepped back a pace and studied me with concern. "Do you know where the glasses are? I'm pouring you a drink."

Aah…we'd raised the boy well. "Glasses are chilling in the freezer. You'll find some wine in the side door of the fridge."

He filled a glass half-full of Chardonnay and handed it to me. I took a sip, and the cold acidity of the wine was both invigorating and calming. "Thanks, sweetie. Say, could you grab a bag of frozen peas?"

He hurried back to inspect the sparse contents of the freezer. "I don't see any peas…how about Brussels sprouts?"

With a smile, I accepted the makeshift ice bag and held it to the back of my head. "Perfect. I don't plan on cooking them."

He leaned against the counter and folded his arms in front of him. Though everyone keeps saying how he's the perfect combination of Terry and me, the truth is he really doesn't look much like either of us. While I'm a strawberry blonde with a nose that's a tad too broad and blue-green eyes that are set a bit too close, Jeff has dark brown hair that brushes eyebrows atop wide blue eyes fringed with thick lashes.

My husband Terry has light brown hair that's beginning to gray at the temples. Since an unfortunate run-in with our old gas grill, he has no eyebrows to speak of, and his nose is rounded like Santa's, a distinguishing feature of every male in his family photo album. Curiously, the "Winters nose" seems to have skipped a generation: Terry likes to joke about Jeff's nose looking more like the mailman's than his.

His Claus-like face isn't Terry's only asset: Not once during our 25 years together has he complained about my Cluster C, and being married to someone who's subject to irrational fears on a daily basis can be quite cumbersome. I'd submit his name for official sainthood, but we're Protestant, so I don't think he's eligible.

I heard a low rumble as the garage door was set into motion. The kitchen door opened with a slam, and keys dropped onto the counter with a clatter. "Amanda?!"

"You're home awfully early—must be a slow news day." Terry works at the Phoenix CBS affiliate as an associate producer. He says that if he's forced to put together one more "cute animal story," he's going to quit. I tell him that I'd take surfboarding pigs and singing dogs over murder and mayhem any day of the week.

He knelt in front of my chair and took my hand. "Panic attack?"

"Uh-huh."

"We should get you checked out at the clinic." He glanced at Jeff. "Your mother was unconscious?"

"She came to just after I got here."

Terry studied my eyes. "That's a first. You've never blacked out before, have you?"

Bracing my palms against the surface of the table, I rose to my feet. "As I was just telling Jeff, I'm fine. And there's no need to get me 'checked out.' I'm going to finish lining these shelves if it takes me all night."

"You've been working on the kitchen since I left this morning." His eyes narrowed as they took in the chaos of the room. "Haven't you?"

"Yes, I have...at least I've been trying. But people kept calling me to see how our move went, the Sun Lakes Welcome Wagon lady came over so I had to stop what I was doing to make some coffee for her, then Aunt Sally forced me to go to McDonalds with her for lunch. Then . . . ."

"Never mind all that. I'm treating you to dinner tonight." He found a Blue Moon and popped it open. "Right after we take you to the clinic. Want a beer, Jeff?"

"Sure. Thanks."

We'd recently moved from our Chandler condo into my dad's house. He'd suffered a heart attack six months earlier at age 84. He died doing what he loved most: playing bocce ball with the guys. Since my mom's death a year before, he'd been saying that he was ready to join her. I had to hand it to my dad: He always said what he meant, and he always meant what he said.

We thought about selling the place, but it has many fond memories and a swimming pool in the backyard. Technically, Sun Lakes is a "lifestyle community"— translated, *golfer's utopia*—that's restricted to residents aged 55 and over, but the board voluntarily allows up to 20 percent of its households to peak somewhere between 40 and 55. So, despite the fact that neither Terry nor I golf—unless you count occasional trips to the mini-putt course over in Mesa—here we are. Sun Lakes, with convoys of speeding golf carts on its roads and lines of penny-counting seniors in its checkout lanes, may not be the Promised Land, but it'll do for now.

Jeff lives in an apartment near ASU's Tempe campus, where he assures us he's studying computer science. He's between girlfriends and jobs at the moment, but he has a best buddy/roommate who also happens to be my godson, Nathan, and a saltwater aquarium that takes up much of his time when he's not in class or at our place raiding the fridge.

I had showered and was in the bedroom changing into something suitable for public scrutiny when the doorbell rang. Through the rear window, I could see Terry and Jeff sipping their beer while sitting on the patio near the pool. They wouldn't have heard the bell. I slid into flip-flops and ran my hands through hair that was still damp. At the front door, I peeked through the side window and saw a uniformed policeman and some guy sporting a ponytail, John Lennon eyeglasses, and a brown suit standing at the entryway and peering up at the palm trees in our front yard. My gaze followed theirs. We hadn't had a chance to set up a landscape service yet, but would overgrown fronds be reason enough for the Sun Lakes HOA to sic the police on us?

In a flash, the Cluster C kicked in to assault my brain with an ever-worsening montage of non-flora scenarios: one of our new neighbors had called to complain about the U-Haul truck that had been parked in our driveway for the past two days; Aunt Sally had crashed her Cadillac into an oil tanker on the way home from dropping me off after lunch; Dinah, Nathan's mother and my best friend, who was due back from Vegas today, was on a flight that had been hijacked by inept terrorists who'd caused the plane to plummet thirty thousand feet into Lake Mead.

I froze for several moments, backed away from the door like Sigourney Weaver backing away from the alien, spun toward the kitchen, and walked through four feet of quicksand to the patio door.

"Dear God in heaven, Terry, the police are here!" I stumbled over the threshold and onto the patio just as brown suit came strolling through the back gate. His officer friend was right behind him.

Brown suit unclipped an ID badge from his lapel and held it out to me. "Detective Roy Staatz, ma'am. Tempe Police Department."

I examined the badge. In all the detective shows, people who skip that step usually live—and sometimes die—to regret it.

Brown suit cleared his throat loudly, either to establish his authority or to express his discomfort at the situation—I wasn't sure which. "We're looking for Jeff Winters."

"He's my son," I exclaimed, looking at Jeff—then Terry.

"I'm investigating a homicide, ma'am. We need to talk to your son."

Chapter Two

My brain took a few seconds to register what I'd just heard and made a clumsy hurdle over the word "homicide" before snapping back to attention. I pictured a route unfolding across the concrete pad in front of me, like footprints appearing one by one on a map in a cartoon, and focused on each step as I moved across the patio to the safe harbor of my family. Clutching Terry's arm with my right hand and Jeff's arm with my left, I was a human hammock teetering between two dependable oaks.

Detective Staatz adjusted his glasses and studied me with concern. I noticed that despite the glasses and the long hair, he didn't resemble John Lennon at all. He looked more like a younger version of Willie Nelson, with fewer wrinkles and without that glazed look his fans seem to find so appealing.

"Mrs. Winters?"

I nodded.

"Are you all right?"

I nodded again.

"Visits from the police tend to make my wife feel a bit shaky," said Terry.

Staatz narrowed his eyes and studied me with concern. "Do the police drop in on you often, Mrs. Winters?"

"Of course not," I said, my eyes threatening to pop out of their sockets despite my efforts to keep them from doing so.

Terry offered an apologetic glance in my direction and said, "Amanda suffers from an anxiety disorder. She—"

I elbowed Terry—just enough, I thought, to remind him that upon first meetings with business acquaintances, Jeff's girlfriends, or officials who had the authority to lock me up for one reason or another, certain skeletons are to remain hidden deep in our closet. Terry clutched his stomach with both hands and gasped, so I guess my jab was not quite as gentle as I'd intended.

Jeff tossed us a look of mild rebuke before addressing Detective Staatz. "You said homicide. Did someone die?" His voice shook, and it occurred to me that I might not be the only member of the Winters family who would be passing out today.

Staatz carried a small electronic pad (an impressive change from the usual spiral notebook detectives used in the movies, I thought). Ignoring Jeff's question for the moment, he squinted at the iPad screen while tapping it to life, then looked up expectantly. "One of your friends was found dead in the Salt River early this morning. Cause of death appears to be drowning, but someone shot him in the head before he died."

Jeff, dragging me down with him, fell numbly onto the edge of his grandmother's floral chaise lounge. "No. God, no...."

"Which one?" I asked.

"Excuse me?" Staatz glanced up from his pad.

"Which friend?" I had already begun to pray, but the answer was the worst possible one.

"Nathan Reynolds."

"There must be some mistake." My voice echoed in my ears as if it were coming from the inside of a cave. Dinah Reynolds and I had met 21 years earlier while we were both in labor and being wheeled up to the intake desk at St. Joseph's Hospital. Dinah and her then-husband, Tom, were Jeff's godparents, and Terry and I were Nathan's. Jeff and Nathan had graduated kindergarten, middle school, and high school together. They shared a birthdate and, for the past three years, an off-campus apartment.

"I'm afraid not, ma'am. His ASU ID card was found on his body."

I buried my face in my hands. I didn't want to lose control in front of strangers, but the tears had a mind of their own and came through in an unstoppable rush.

Detective Staatz said, "I'm sorry, ma'am."

The uniformed officer, whose name tag identified him as Jerry Bloedel, turned away and pretended to study with interest the stucco wall that enclosed our backyard.

Terry said, "The boys grew up together. Dinah—Nathan's mother—is a good friend."

"We tried to reach Mrs. Reynolds on her cell phone, but there was no answer," said Staatz. He glanced at Jeff. "We found the note you left for Nathan in your apartment saying you'd be here helping your parents unpack at their new home. You know Nathan's mother?"

"Yeah," said Jeff, staring at his feet. "She's in Vegas."

"It wasn't a pleasure trip," I said, as if it mattered. "She goes to a real estate conference every January." My explanation continued in staccato bursts between sobs and sharp intakes of air. "Her plane is probably just now—getting into Sky Harbor. You didn't—leave a message...."

"No, no, we don't leave messages in these cases. Can you tell me anything about Nathan's father?"

"He left ten years ago, and no one's heard from him since," said Terry.

Staatz shifted a bit on his feet. "What did he do? What was his line of work?"

"Corporate law," I said.

Staatz made some notes, then looked up expectantly. "Do you know where he is…how he can be reached?"

Terry shook his head. "His family doesn't even know where he is."

Dinah hadn't been able to make peace with that particular heartbreak, at least not sufficiently to put closure on the marriage. Now this…

"What about the law firm he worked for? Would someone there know his current address?"

"The firm was dissolved years ago."

Staatz made another note and fixed his gaze on Jeff. "When did you last see Nathan?"

Jeff wiped tears from his face, an abrupt gesture that conveyed anger more than sadness. His best friend, the son of *my* best friend, was dead. I didn't blame him for being angry—I was angry, too.

Jeff rubbed his face fiercely and said, his voice breaking, "Yesterday, maybe around four or four-thirty. He took off on his bike to meet his girlfriend. He said they were going to a movie." I lifted a hand to brush an ever-present shock of stray hair from Jeff's eyes, and he pushed it away.

"Can you give me the name of the girl?"

"Danielle Palmer."

"Do you know where she lives?"

"Somewhere in Scottsdale with her mom. I don't know where her dad lives…but I'm pretty sure he's on the faculty at ASU Polytechnic."

Staatz lowered his head to stare over the top of his glasses at Jeff. "I'd like you to come down to the station…it shouldn't take much more than an hour or so."

I knew what was going to come next: Staatz would put Jeff in a dark, airless, little room and barrage him with questions until he confessed. I watch all the cop shows: Remove the suspect from his comfort zone, isolate him, and drive him crazy with accusations until he breaks.

"You're not accusing Jeff of murder!" I said, or assumed I'd said. I was under the impression, at least, that my lips had moved. They'd moved, all right, but my voice had somehow gone missing.

"Ma'am?"

I licked my lips and repeated the words, this time aloud.

"No, ma'am, I'm sure not accusing anyone of anything."

Another wave of tears flooded Jeff's eyes. Suddenly, seated on the chaise lounge next to me was the little boy we used to call Jeffy, a ten-year-old in Oshkosh B'gosh overalls and a Batman T-shirt. I blinked and looked again to see the fully grown young man who'd just had his world come crashing down on him.

"You didn't worry when Nathan failed to come home last night?" asked Staatz.

"We don't check up on each other like that. I mean, Nate had a girlfriend...."

"Can you tell me where you were last night? What you were doing?"

Jeff gritted his teeth, a habit he'd inherited from me and which surfaced during times of stress. "Nothing much...I went to Barnes & Noble."

"Were you alone?"

"Yeah. I got a gift certificate for Christmas, and I wanted to use it."

"Did you buy anything?"

"I couldn't find anything I liked."

"What time did you get back to the apartment?"

"I dunno. It was late…after ten, maybe."

Staatz studied Jeff's face. I could tell the detective was considering the possibility that my son was somehow involved in Nathan's death. I pressed my eyes shut and wished Staatz away, like the boy in that old *Twilight Zone* episode who wished annoying people into the cornfield, but when I opened them he was still there. This was really happening. My godson was dead, his young life snuffed out by person or persons unknown for reasons as yet undetermined. By sheer force of will, Terry and I'd managed to keep our own son out of harm's way for 21 years, but stronger measures—fierce, tangible measures—would likely be needed now that murder had entered our lives.

Staatz licked his finger as though he were about to leaf through a book and scrolled to a new page in his iPad. "Can you think of anyone who would want to hurt Nathan? Anyone who would want him dead?"

"No. No one."

Staatz weighed Jeff's answer with a thoughtful nod. "We just need to finalize this part of the investigation. Our computers, phones, records, things we need to check…they're all at the station." He flashed a humorless smile and tapped off his iPad. "I'm still getting used to this thing."

Jeff's face blanched. "Are you going to arrest me?"

"No, no…like I said, we just need to ask you a few more questions so we can move on."

"Can we drive him to the station?" asked Terry.

Staatz shrugged. "Sure. I don't care how he gets there, as long as he gets there."

*****

The Tempe PD substation where Staatz was headquartered occupied a building in the southwest corner of ASU's main campus in the university's former R.O.T.C. headquarters. While checking campus crime statistics prior to Jeff's enrollment, I'd learned that the Tempe force frequently assists the ASU force, particularly with respect to the more horrendous crimes committed on university premises or those perpetrated on its students off-campus.

We walked through an open wrought-iron gate and into a Spanish-style courtyard featuring a three-tiered stone fountain surrounded by ceramic pots of aloe. Oversized pillars stood sentry on either side of twin oak doors. In contrast, the interior looked just like any other office building. There were three desks with computers and standard-issue black phones. Gun-metal green filing cabinets lined white walls that reflected a dirty gray hue under the fluorescent lighting.

We checked in with a uniformed officer. Staatz and the cop who'd accompanied him to our home strode in through the front door, which closed behind them with a slam of finality that caused me to shiver.

"You got here ahead of us," the detective said, his voice light-hearted, obviously meant to put us at ease. "I hope you didn't break any speed limits."

Staatz's kindly intentions notwithstanding, I ignored his attempt at humor. "Have you talked to Nathan's mother yet?"

"A support team is on its way to Mrs. Reynolds' home right now. Her plane touched down about half an hour ago."

I closed my eyes in an effort to erase the image of Dinah's face as she received news of her child's death. The best thought I could summon at this moment was a selfish one: *I* wasn't the mother who was about to hear the unthinkable. *My* son hadn't been the one found floating in the Salt River. Life was full of ironies. I had every right to be happy and thankful that Jeff was alive and healthy. Still, I couldn't be too happy or too thankful, because my best friend had just lost her only son.

Chapter Three

Staatz escorted Jeff into an office adjoining the main room. The front-desk officer pointed at a row of orange plastic chairs flanking the front entrance. "You can wait over there if you want."

After twenty minutes of physical discomfort that made our mental distress all the more unbearable, Terry and I went outside to wait in the courtyard. I don't think I took a full breath until the moment I saw Jeff, hands in his pockets, come shuffling through the front doors of the building. I tried to read his face, but there was nothing there to give me the slightest hint as to what he'd just been through. A part of me had been positive that Staatz, regardless of his assurances to the contrary, was going to arrest him, and that we'd have to watch our son, handcuffed and being led out of the building to a waiting squad car that would escort him to a high-security prison.

I waited for Jeff to say something, but he walked past us and out through the gate without a word. I wanted desperately to ask what the "few more questions" were that Staatz had needed to ask him, but Terry gave me a cautionary look to which I reluctantly yielded.

At the car, Terry gave Jeff's back an encouraging pat. "Let's get Mom to the walk-in clinic—then we can get some dinner."

"I'm not hungry," said Jeff, his voice broken.

"Neither am I," said Terry. "But we have to eat."

"Please, can we skip the clinic?" I pleaded in a tone that was alarmingly close to a whine. "I told you, I'm fine." The last thing I wanted to do was wait for hours only to be informed that I suffered from a chronic panic disorder. No surprise there. All I wanted to do right now was to cocoon with my family in the comfort of familiar surroundings.

"Amanda, your father died of a heart attack."

"He was 84! And he ate three eggs and a half-pound of bacon for breakfast every morning. Besides, as you well know, I was adopted. Given the right genes and a little luck, I could live to be a hundred."

Terry opened the front passenger door and waved me in. "I'm not in the mood to argue with you." I could tell there was no more room for discussion, because he'd assumed the tone of a minister admonishing one of his congregants.

I managed, at least, to persuade him to take me to "The Little Clinic" at Fry's Market rather than to Sun Lake's Urgent Care, where the waiting room would no doubt be overflowing with wheezing, sneezing, and hacking hordes of people who might give me some illness that I could actually die from. After I checked in at the counter, Terry dragged Jeff off to explore the store's inventory of grills and patio furniture.

The grouping of chairs in the waiting area, strategically placed so that patients could spend quality time gazing upon shelf after shelf of over-the-counter drugs, diet aids, and personal care products, was empty except for an elderly gentleman sipping coffee from a Styrofoam cup. Add a top hat and a walking stick, and he'd be perfect for the role of Ebenezer Scrooge in the Sun Lakes' Players next performance of *A Christmas Carol*. I sat down across from him and smiled. "Are you waiting to see the doctor?"

"You're danged right I'm waiting for the doctor—and I'll have you know that I was here first!" he said.

Before I could think of a suitable response, Scrooge was summoned to the examination room. I offered thanks for small favors and settled in to read the previous year's Easter edition of *Good Housekeeping*. An hour later, Terry and Jeff returned, just as a smiling redhead in a lab coat opened the exam room door and called my name. Scrooge pushed his way past her into the waiting area and snarled at me, "You're danged lucky you don't have a prostate, lady. You'd be crap out of luck."

Inside the exam room, the doctor patted the top of a table covered in fresh white paper. "Have a seat, Mrs. Winters."

As she wrapped the blood pressure cuff around my arm, I felt my heart begin to pound in my chest. I used some deep-breathing exercises in an effort to slow the rate to normal; a racing pulse would result in a lousy reading that would also get me a stern warning and a prescription for pills that would, no doubt, do nothing but give me a nasty skin rash. During the EKG, I started to feel dizzy and gripped both sides of the exam table to keep from floating away.

The doctor frowned at me with concern. "You okay?"

"I will be in a minute," I said. "It's been a rough day."

"Nothing serious, I hope?"

"Just about as serious as it gets."

On my way out, I glanced at the printout she'd handed me. Under "Preliminary Diagnosis," she'd written *acute panic episode*. What did I tell you?

Terry and Jeff were waiting for me when I stepped out of the exam room. "I'm fine, just like I said." I handed Terry the receipt from my appointment. "Sorry.

She insisted on doing an EKG and a blood work-up...a lipid panel, she called it. She thought I should have one, since I've never yet had the pleasure."

We headed for the car, and Terry pushed the receipt into his pocket without looking at it. "When will you get the results? What did she say?"

"The EKG was fine...she said my blood pressure was slightly elevated. The panel results should be ready within a few days. But that's neither here nor there. I really need you to drop me off at Dinah's right now."

"I think you should give her a few hours—I'll take you over after dinner." He started the car and said, "We have to drive around back to customer pick-up. I found a grill."

After helping Terry load the grill into the trunk, Jeff settled in the backseat and silently stared out through the window. At a stoplight, I turned to follow his gaze to the sky above the mountains, where a red and blue Southwest jet cruised past a setting sun that peeked around clouds limned with colors ranging from coral to vermillion. Jeff looked as if he wished for nothing more than to be on that plane, whatever its destination. I wanted to be sitting back there with him, to take him into my arms and hold onto him the way I used to when he was little, when he'd come home crying after falling off his scooter or because some older kids wouldn't let him play dodgeball with the group. But the best thing I could do for him now, I knew, was to quash my maternal instincts and respect his privacy by letting him alone to mourn the loss of his friend, wrestle with his thoughts, and reflect on whatever talking points had been the basis of his conversation with Detective Staatz.

*****

During a quick dinner at the Cottonwood Café, one of my dad's old haunts, Jeff asked if he could spend a few nights at our place. "It would be kind of creepy to be alone right now, you know?"

We stopped at the apartment to feed his fish and to pick up some of his things. In the dimly lit third-floor hallway, Jeff moved to insert his key in the lock, and the door swung open a few inches. Terry immediately nudged him aside and peered through the opening. After listening for a few moments and hearing no sound from inside, he pushed the door open wide.

Jeff brushed past Terry and took a few steps into the apartment before stopping in his tracks. "What the heck!"

Even considering the fact that college kids had been living there, the apartment was a mess. In the living room, cushions had been pulled off the red plaid sofa and scattered here and there. Books had been pulled from stacks of plastic crates that had served as shelves. In the kitchen, drawers and cupboards were open, their contents spread across the counters and on the floor. The doors of every appliance hung open: the oven, the refrigerator, and freezer…even the microwave. In each of the two bedrooms, bedding had been ripped apart and tossed aside, and cases had been torn from all the pillows. Dresser drawers were open, and shirts, socks, and underwear had been tossed willy-nilly.

"Should we call 9-1-1?" I asked, afraid that whoever had done this was still in the apartment and poised to attack—from a closet or maybe from behind the shower curtain.

"No," said Terry. "Too late for that...whoever did this is long gone. We'll use the regular police number to call this in."

Two uniforms from the Tempe PD arrived within 15 minutes. "It doesn't look like a break-in," said Officer Judith Harvey, a petite brunette of about thirty. "The lock's intact." She made some notes in a small black notebook and peered at Jeff. "Do you ever leave the front door unlocked?"

"Sometimes, I guess…"

She shook her head in disapproval. "You need to be more careful. Do you all live here?"

"Just me and my roommate," said Jeff. "These are my parents."

I could tell he was debating whether he should correct his initial response, given Nathan's death, but he thought better of it and ended it there.

After pausing to consider it for a moment, I decided that something should be said, if only in the interest of full disclosure. "My son's roommate, Nathan Reynolds, was murdered last night."

Officer Harvey's partner, Ronald McNeary, a giant of a man with straw-colored hair, placed a hand on his holstered gun and assumed a posture of defense. I guess the word "murdered" has that effect on some people. He gave Officer Harvey a furtive glance, as though he were afraid to take his eyes off us, and said, "Roy Staatz is working that case."

"We'll give him a call," replied Harvey. "There's probably no connection—this is our third call-in to the building this week—but he'll want to check things out just the same."

The officers did a walk-through of the apartment with Jeff, taking each room one at a time, to determine whether anything was missing. The big-screen TV in the living room was left untouched, as well as Jeff's laptop and some cash he'd kept in a desk drawer.

"There's no computer in this room," said Harvey as she emerged from Nathan's bedroom. "I assume your roommate had one?"

"Nate took his laptop with him last night," said Jeff. "He always carried it with him."

"I suggest you stay somewhere else for a while...until Detective Staatz gives you the all-clear," said McNeary. "You can take clothes, toothbrush, and whatever other personal effects you'll need, but leave everything else. Staatz will probably want to get a forensics team in here."

McNeary and Harvey waited in the hallway outside the apartment while Jeff and Terry packed some things. I walked into Nathan's room and cleared my mind, trying to absorb some remnant of the young man he'd been. They say that after we die our electrical energy lives on in the physical realm, but all I felt inside that room was a cold emptiness. An old picture of Nathan and his parents standing in front of a Christmas tree, its frame broken, was on the floor. I picked it up and pressed the pieces together as best I could before placing it flat on the dresser.

Jeff came into the room and stood next to me. "I keep thinking that this is some crazy mistake and that Nate will come walking in at any minute."

"I know...me too." I hitched a sigh. "Are you all set?"

"Yeah. I just have to check the nitrate levels in the aquarium. The fish are acting weird."

"Well, they're fish...they *are* weird."

In Jeff's bedroom, Terry checked the windows and adjusted the blinds. "We'll leave a few lamps on," he said. "No use inviting more trouble."

From the sofa, Terry and I watched as Jeff removed a sample of water from the aquarium, transferred it to a glass jar, and dropped liquid from two tiny plastic vials into it before inserting a test strip. "Water seems fine," he said, and bent down to examine the aquarium more closely. "Hey...what's this doing in here?" He reached into a bottom corner of the tank and pulled a metal container the size of a cigar box from behind a large mass of coral reef. Bits of disturbed gravel swirled up into a miniature sandstorm, turning the water cloudy and causing the fish to go berserk. "So this is why they were acting up."

"Where did it come from?" I asked.

"It's the box Nate found in his mom's garage last week," he said.

"Why would he have put it in your aquarium?"

"I dunno. He said there were just some old notes and emails that belonged to his dad." He tugged on the lid to open it. "There's no lock...it's totally jammed shut."

"We'd better take it along and turn it over to Detective Staatz," said Terry. "Nathan must have thought that the papers inside that box were important enough that someone would come looking for them." He took a last look around the ransacked apartment. "And it looks like he may have been right."

Chapter Four

Jeff stashed the box in his backpack, and Officers McNeary and Harvey saw us safely to our PT Cruiser. Terry and I agreed that it was time we headed over to Dinah's. At the entrance to Ocotillo Springs, we pulled up to the security gate, entered Dinah's code, and continued to her house, a stucco villa situated on the edge of a small man-made lake. Smaller and far more exclusive than Sun Lakes, Ocotillo Springs edges the northwest border of Chandler. Warm light peeked around the edges of the blinds, all of which were drawn. A car that looked vaguely familiar was parked in the driveway.

I reached for the door handle and turned to Terry. "Wait here a minute. Once Dinah comes to the door, you can leave. I'll give you a call when it's time to pick me up."

We have only one car. It makes sense, since one of the fringe benefits of my panic disorder is a fear of driving. Being behind the wheel of a car in the midst of any kind of moving traffic assaults my senses to the point that I'm unable to filter out the things that don't matter (like traffic flow on a bridge overpass or the clatter of a train on tracks running parallel to the road), rendering me incapable of dealing with the things that do matter (like maintaining a constant speed or remembering where the brake pedal is). My driving phobia is also the reason why I work from home as a freelance copy editor. I proofread and edit all kinds of documents, from short stories and journal articles to college essays and dissertations. It doesn't pay all that much, and there are no benefits per se, but the work is usually interesting, I get to set my own schedule, and there's no risk of killing myself or someone else by having a panic attack while behind the wheel of a moving vehicle.

As I walked up the path to Dinah's front door, I mentally rehearsed what I would say to her. Nearly every possible phrase or word I considered sounded trite, and all were painfully inadequate. I decided to wing it. I rang the doorbell and glanced over my shoulder in hopes of garnering some moral support from Terry. It was getting dark, but I could tell he was turned toward the backseat and talking earnestly to Jeff. Just as well. Our son needed moral support even more than I did right now.

The door opened. "Hello, Amanda."

"Pastor Mike. I didn't expect to see you here."

Michael Ansdale was the senior pastor of Blessed Trinity Church, where Dinah's family and mine were long-time members, and where Jeff and Nathan had been baptized. Nathan's funeral would take place there.

He stepped outside and closed the door softly behind him. "Dinah's parents called me from Tucson. They asked me to look in on her." He shook his head sadly. "It seems just yesterday that Jeff and Nathan were confirmed...such a tragedy."

"Can you tell her I'm here?"

With some discomfort, he gazed up at the stars. "She knows you're here, Amanda. She's asked me to tell you she's not ready to talk to anyone just yet."

Not ready to talk? Are you kidding me? We'd been friends for 21 years.

"Are you sure?"

"Be patient with her…I'm sure she'll come around soon. I'll ask her to call you when she decides the time is right."

I gulped and swallowed air. "Thank you, Pastor." He stepped back inside and started to close the door, but I reached out to block it with my hand. "Wait. How is she?"

"Not the best, I'm afraid. You can imagine what she's going through right now."

"Will you tell her I'm here for her? Whatever she needs...anything."

"Of course."

I turned and walked back to the Cruiser like someone walking to the gallows. I'd been so caught up with planning what I was going to say to Dinah that it had never occurred to me she wouldn't want to talk to me. I was her best friend, and best friends comforted each other during times of distress and sorrow. The last time I checked the job description, that was one of the main responsibilities.

"Amanda?"

I stopped and turned, hopeful that Dinah had changed her mind. "Yes?"

"I'll see you in church tomorrow morning?"

I nodded, not caring whether or not he saw my response in the dark.

When I pulled open the car door and got in, Terry asked, "Aren't you staying?"

"Apparently not. According to Pastor Mike, Dinah isn't ready to talk to me."

Jeff's words licked over the backseat like flames. "It's not you, Mom. Mrs. Reynolds thinks it's my fault Nate's dead. She probably hates me. Friends are supposed to have each other's backs...but I didn't have Nate's back. Not at all!" His sob was raw and painful to hear. "Maybe it *is* my fault he's dead."

"Jeff, don't…" I started. I stopped there, because, despite the fact that Jeff's statement had no validity whatsoever, I'd been wondering if Dinah was holding Jeff—and by extension, me—at least partly responsible for Nathan's death. I tried to reverse the situation in my mind: Would I blame Dinah if Terry and I had gone on vacation and returned to find Jeff dead? The answer was hazy.

"Let's go home," Terry said, and started up the car.

*****

I made up the bed in the guest room while Terry and Jeff settled in front of the TV. When I joined them in the living room, Terry, his hands folded across his midsection and his feet propped up on the ottoman, was snoring softly while Jeff stared at a *Scooby Doo* rerun.

"We used to watch these together, remember?" I said, and sat down next to him.

"Yeah. They're classics."

"Come into the kitchen with me a minute…I want to ask you something."

He eyed me with suspicion. "Why can't we just talk here?"

I glanced at Terry. "Because I don't think you want your dad to wake up and hear what it is I'm going to ask you."

In the kitchen, I motioned for Jeff to have a seat. The mess from earlier that day was, of course, still there. No elves had crept in through the windows to put things in order while I was busy trying to keep the rest of my life from falling apart. Maybe bringing Jeff into the room had been a bad idea: I didn't want the chaos of the kitchen to further aggravate the psychological chaos we both were suffering.

"What do you know that you aren't telling us?"

After avoiding my gaze for a few awkward moments, Jeff faced me head-on. "Seriously?"

I sat down at the table across from him and swept crumpled wads of tissue paper aside. "When is the last time you actually went to a bookstore to buy a book? A year ago, maybe two? Jeff, you've had your Kindle for a year. Dad and I gave it to you last Christmas, remember?"

When he began to squirm uncomfortably in his chair, I knew I had him where I wanted him. Still, it gave me no satisfaction.

"There's something you're not saying, which, in this case, is the same thing as lying. And lying about a crime is more than enough to get you arrested."

He pressed back into the chair and stretched his long legs out to the max. "I didn't go to the bookstore last night," he said. "I followed Nate." His gaze met mine with an intensity that was challenging and penitent at the same time. "At least I tried to. I lost him."

"What do you mean, you lost him?"

"I was able to follow him to Mill Avenue, but he was on his bike, and I was in my car. I got caught at a red light, and I lost him."

"Why were you following him in the first place?" I rose from the table and walked to the cabinet, where I'd stowed a bottle of Merlot. This conversation called for a serious red.

"Nate said he was meeting someone who might be able to tell him where his dad is…and you know—why he left. I said I'd go along with him, but he brushed me off."

I poured some wine into a water tumbler, the only clean glass I could find. "That doesn't explain why you were following him."

"Nate found a bunch of old emails some nut job sent his dad ten years ago…you know, just before he took off. He found them in this box in his mom's garage last week, along with some notes from a case his dad had been working on and some other stuff. I figured that if this was the same creep that sent those emails, Nate might be in for some trouble. I mean, if the guy knew something about his dad, why couldn't he just tell Nate over the phone?"

I took a protracted sip, enjoying the wine's comforting warmth. "Did you tell any of this to Detective Staatz when he questioned you at the police station?"

"I couldn't, Mom. I totally freaked out—I thought he'd arrest me if I told him I followed Nate. I mean, I followed him, and the next thing, he turns up dead."

"So what *did* you tell him?"

"Pretty much the same thing I told him earlier this morning." He buried his face in his hands. "Man…I don't even know what to do now."

I reached across the table and touched his arm. "Well, I do. We're going into the living room, and you're going to tell your dad what you've just told me. Then, first thing tomorrow, you're going to call Detective Staatz, and this time you're going to tell him the truth."

Chapter Five
Sunday

I filled a mug with strong coffee, then sat and stared at the phone for ten minutes before actually punching in Dinah's number. I let it ring until her voice mail message came on, but hung up without leaving one of my own. I knew she was there, watching my number flash in the little plastic window. I could feel it.

I need to mention here...despite the fact that most people today seem glued to their phones 24/7, quite the opposite is true for me. Particularly on my worst days, the phone is not my friend: Its ring often prompts me to run through the house like a deranged Tattoo, Ricardo Montalban's *Fantasy Island* sidekick, yelling, "The phone, the phone!"

This behavior, I'm told, stems from my avoidant personality disorder, which is also associated with my tendency to expect the worst possible thing to happen at any given moment. When the phone rings, I automatically assume that someone is calling with bad news: a spot discovered on an x-ray, a fatal accident, a wayward meteor hitting the TV station during Terry's shift... It's odd to think that, yesterday, some of the worst news I could ever have imagined decided to bypass the phone and came straight to my door.

Jeff, his face pale except for the bruise-like shadows beneath his eyes, plodded into the kitchen. He was wearing the Christmas PJs I'd given him, a traditional gift dating back to his infancy: This year's ensemble featured green plaid flannels with an appliqué of Han

Solo and Chewbacca toasting each other with reindeer-head mugs. He poured himself a cup of coffee. "Is there any cereal?"

"Somewhere. Let me look."

"I got it." He held the box up and examined it. "Bran Flakes?"

"Sorry. We weren't expecting anyone under the age of forty for breakfast."

"Whatever. I'm really not hungry anyway."

I watched him as he poured heaping spoonfuls of sugar and milk into his coffee mug. "Did you get any sleep at all last night?"

"Naw...I couldn't stop thinking about Nate."

"It's going to be rough for a while. I promise you, though, that each day will get a little better."

"I hope it happened quick," he said. "God, I hope he didn't feel anything..."

"I'm sure he didn't," I said, praying that it was true.

I wanted to give Jeff's mind a chance to clear out the horrific images that must now be a significant part of his existence, both waking and sleeping, so I decided to make the call to Staatz myself. Though it was Sunday and I trusted that even homicide detectives got a day of rest now and then, I called him at the number on the business card he'd given me. As expected, I had to leave a message.

I studied the empty kitchen cupboards and all the boxes that waited to be unpacked. It was strange, how important freshly-lined shelves had seemed yesterday; today, I had other priorities. I stood at the patio door, sipping coffee and examining the orange trees in the yard. A lot of the fruit had gone to the birds or dropped, overripe and bursting, to the ground. Next year would offer a better harvest. I smiled to see that some new blossoms had already popped and watched, mesmerized, as a hummingbird darted and whirred among the branches to take advantage of that fact.

I cast a hopeful look in Jeff's direction. "Will you be coming to church with us?"

"Naw, I don't think so. Officer Harvey's meeting me over at the apartment; I need to pick up some more stuff and check on the fish."

I resisted an urge to tell him that food for his soul might, at this point in time, be more beneficial for him than food for Benny the clownfish or Brutus the seahorse. Instead, I tried to find the hummingbird again, but it must have moved along its route and into the neighbor's yard.

A sharp rapping on the patio door caused me to jump, sending my coffee sloshing over the rim of my mug and onto the floor. A small nose was pressed flat against the pane, and a pair of eyes that were magnified to an alarming size through thick round lenses peered in at me: Aunt Sally. With permed blond hair that flipped up at the ends in wispy clouds of frizz and a mouth that suggested a square, my dad's baby sister was the image of Phyllis Diller before the commencement of plastic surgery. I cringed when I noticed she had the Sunday edition of the *Phoenix Republic* tucked under her arm. Since she'd already seen me, I had no choice but to open the door.

"Aunt Sally! What brings you here so early on a Sunday morning?" Of course I knew very well what had brought her: A picture of Nathan was prominently displayed on the front page of the paper.

She unfolded it and poked the picture with her pointer finger. "Your godchild is murdered, and you don't call me?!" Her eyes bulged out of their sockets with even more intensity than usual.

"I'm sorry. I didn't think…"

"Humph. Tell me something I don't know."

Jeff issued a little cough to announce his presence and said, "How's Arnold doing?"

Aunt Sally had named her car "Arnold" for reasons she refused to talk about. Someday, she promised us, she'd tell us that story.

"Purrs like a kitten and rides like butter," she said. She trotted over to Jeff and kissed the top of his head. "I didn't expect to see you, Jeffy. I'm so glad you're all right." She turned to me. "It could have been this one, you know. They lived in the same apartment."

I stifled a sigh. "Yes, I know they lived in the same apartment, but…."

"The killer could just as easily have murdered Nathan with Jeffy right there to witness the whole thing, and then shot him to death, too. We could be looking at your son's picture on the front page right here alongside poor Nathan's."

I observed Jeff's face turning progressively whiter. "Aunt Sally, please…"

"Amanda, the shower's all yours," said Terry as he walked into the kitchen. "You'd better hurry. We have to leave in half an hour." What a guy, forever coming to my rescue in one way or another. "Morning, Aunt Sally. Can I pour you some coffee?"

I excused myself and hurried off to get ready for church before I could be inundated with additional opinions, questions, or hypotheses about Nathan's death. I felt a bit guilty at leaving Terry and Jeff to fend for themselves, but what the heck…they were grown men who'd surely be able to handle even the likes of Aunt Sally.

*****

After church, Terry turned on his cell phone in the vestibule and checked it for messages, but there was nothing. Since I wasn't in the mood for pious platitudes after last night's interception by Pastor Mike, I steered us toward a side exit in an attempt to elude him. He spotted us, however, and used the knowledge he'd gained as an avid Cardinals fan (his familiar red jersey was often spotted sticking up through the collar of his white robe on Sunday mornings)—to block our escape.

"The medical examiner will be releasing Nathan's body sometime Tuesday," he said. "The funeral is scheduled for Thursday. I thought you'd want to know."

I mumbled my thanks and urged Terry through the door and into the parking lot. Dinah hadn't been sitting in her usual pew, but I hadn't expected to see her there. She'd likely already moved on to the stage of grieving that was all about anger. I was pretty sure that, despite her refusal to talk to me, God was the one feeling the brunt of her rage right now.

*****

Terry and I walked into the kitchen to find Jeff sitting at the table and trying to pry the lid off Tom Reynolds' metal box with one of my good butter knives.

"What are you doing?" I asked.

"Trying to open this box."

Terry frowned. "I thought we agreed to turn it over to Detective Staatz."

"Yeah, but don't you want to see those emails before we do that?"

"It's not our business, Jeff."

"Nate hid this stuff in my aquarium," said Jeff. "I think he'd want me to see them."

Terry tossed me a questioning look, and I nodded. He went out to the garage to find a tool more suitable for prying the lids off rusty metal boxes, and, minutes later, the three of us were staring down at a stack of old papers.

Terry picked up the papers and began to unfold them one at a time. "This is a page from Tom Reynolds' old Day Planner." Leafing through the stack, he gave each of the papers a cursory examination. "…and some of Tom's old case notes…and these are printouts of emails, all addressed to Tom."

I snatched one of the emails from Terry's hand and read it aloud. *"If you don't do something to stop the monster you work for, you're as guilty as he is."*

Terry read another that said, *"Stop the killing now or you'll regret it."*

"What's the signature on yours?" I asked.

"Anthony Hunter."

"That's the signature on this one, too," I said.

We unfolded each of the emails—there were twelve—arranged them by date, and read them in order. All of them were from Anthony Hunter, and each was more threatening than the one before.

The last one said, *"You MURDERED my wife… and someone is going to PAY. An eye for an eye. I WARNED YOU."*

Chapter Six

Detective Staatz called to say he'd be over shortly after noon. We settled in the living room in a loose circle around the coffee table. In the center of the table was Tom Reynolds' metal box, which we regarded in awed silence as though it were some mysterious relic from an Indiana Jones movie.

The detective was the first to speak. He looked away from the box and, in classic private-eye fashion, carefully studied the room. "Interesting décor," he said.

"This house belonged to my parents," I explained. "We just moved in and haven't had a chance to do much of anything yet." The living room walls, carpeting, and drapes, as well as the landscaping rock in the front and back yards, had all been done in various shades of blue. "The Smurf house," Terry and I had jokingly called the place. "My mother said all the blue made the house feel cooler, even in the middle of an Arizona August."

Staatz nodded. "Makes sense, I suppose." He accepted the coffee I offered him and got down to business. "Jeff, do you have any idea who trashed your apartment?"

"No. I mean, it's not like we had anything worth stealing."

"Well, someone apparently thought you did." Staatz studied Jeff for a long moment and glanced at me before turning his attention back to him. "Maybe something in this box you found?"

"Maybe. I don't know."

"Your mom said that you had something to tell me. Does it have anything to do with Nathan's murder, or with the break-in?"

"Yeah...I'm beginning to think so."

Careful to avoid eye contact with Staatz, Jeff related his story...how he'd followed Nathan Friday night and then lost him on Mill Avenue. "Last week, Nate found this box with some stuff in his mom's garage...a page from his dad's old work calendar, some notes, and some crazy emails a guy had sent him just before he took off."

"A man named Anthony Hunter," I interjected.

"Anyway," Jeff continued, "Nate got hold of someone who his dad was supposed to meet with that last day. He said he was going to try and find out what happened...why his dad just disappeared, you know, without a word."

"And did Nathan actually meet with anyone the night he was murdered?"

"I don't know. Like I said, I lost track of him on Mill. After that, I gave up and just came home."

Staatz frowned, opened the box, and surveyed its contents. "Tell me why you think I'd be interested in any of this."

"There are notes in there that are from a case Tom was working on when he disappeared," I said. "And he must have included the calendar page because the people scheduled for that day were all somehow connected to it. We read the emails. This Anthony Hunter was sending some pretty nasty threats to Nathan's father. Hunter was one of the people who Tom was scheduled to meet with on that day. Maybe Nathan confronted him about it and..."

Staatz cut me off at the pass. "And you think Hunter may have killed Nathan to cover up the fact that he'd scared Tom Reynolds off with a few threatening emails ten years ago." He used both hands to smooth his hair, which hung loose to his shoulders today. "That's quite a leap, Mrs. Winters."

I glanced at Terry, hoping to borrow a modicum of his self-confidence, but he made a point of looking everywhere but in my direction. I was on my own. "You'd better read those emails, Detective. You may want to consider the possibility that Tom wasn't 'scared off' ten years ago. Hunter was angry…maybe angry enough to commit murder."

Though Staatz didn't verbally respond to my premise, he did seem to mull over the possibility before replacing the contents of the box and snapping the lid shut. "I'll be taking this in as evidence." He directed a punitive gaze at Jeff. "Is there anything else you should be telling me?"

"No. That's all I know."

"I have every right to arrest you for obstruction of justice. Do you understand?"

"Yes, sir."

Rising to leave, Staatz lifted the box from the table and said to no one in particular, "Say maybe Nathan did meet with this Hunter fellow to confront him about these emails—assuming Hunter had something to do with Tom Reynolds' disappearance—maybe even killed him. That could be motive enough for this Hunter guy to kill Nathan, too." He looked at each of us and jabbed a finger in the air. "You didn't hear any of that."

"I didn't hear a thing," I said weakly. "None of us did."

"Hunter might have assumed that Nathan would bring the emails to the meeting," said Terry, "but since Nathan didn't have the emails on him…"

"…Hunter would have come looking for them at the boys' apartment," I finished.

Staatz turned to leave. "I should be getting the forensics report from the break-in before the end of the week. Maybe we'll at least be able to come up with some prints." He turned to Jeff. "I've officially cleared your apartment, but if I were you, I'd stay put right here for a while."

*****

I checked again for a message from Dinah, but there still was nothing. I decided to make a pan of lasagna to take over that evening. Italian food was her favorite: She might be able to reject me, but never in a million years would she be able to say no to my lasagna. I'd throw in some garlic bread and a green salad for good measure.

On the way to Dinah's, I sat silently next to Terry, my body rigid and my mind numb. I clung to a plastic container of green salad as though it were a lifesaver someone had tossed to save me from drowning. I had gone all out: hearts of romaine, arugula, sunburst tomatoes, and homemade croutons dusted with grated Asiago cheese. In the backseat, a Fry's shopping bag containing my lasagna and a foil-wrapped garlic loaf was sending out mouth-watering aromas. There was no way on God's green earth that Dinah wasn't going to let me in this time.

With the handle of the shopping bag clutched in my right hand and the plastic container of salad in my left, I made my way along the path to the front door. I set the shopping bag down and rang the doorbell. I dropped the salad when the door opened and Dinah, or rather a ghost-version of Dinah, her face white with dark circles under her eyes, appeared. We didn't say anything…just fell into each other's arms, sobbing heart-wrenching, guttural sounds, the only language capable of expressing our feelings at that moment. Tears pouring down my cheeks, I threw my arms around her shoulders and hugged her more tightly than my present strength could account for. I stepped back to see the shadow of a smile on her face, and I knew then that we were going to be all right—maybe not for a while, yet—but there was no question in my mind that our friendship would survive even this horror, the death of her child at the hands of a murderer.

Terry and I had discussed whether or not I should bring up the subject of the box containing Tom's notes, the calendar page, and the threatening emails, and we decided that doing so would needlessly add to the already overwhelming burden of Nathan's death. I considered the question: Her son's murder notwithstanding, would Dinah want to be presented with the possibility that Tom had also been murdered, his body buried somewhere in the desert, or would that idea be even more difficult to contemplate than the belief that he'd abandoned her and Nathan?

I pushed the question to that dark place in my mind that holds all the other questions I'll have to face someday, and said, "I brought lasagna."

She bent down to retrieve the container of salad, and I signaled to Terry that it was okay for him to leave. In the foyer, rustic but elegant with its tall beamed ceiling and terrazzo flooring, I lingered to admire a beautifully framed oil painting, a desert scene created by a well-known Phoenix artist, and to inhale the sweet fragrance of roses in a vase on the black marble table. I experienced a twinge of covetousness: Dinah's home was a far cry from my newly acquired Smurf house. The twinge lasted only a second, when I remembered that I still had my son, and Dinah no longer had hers.

I followed her through a living room decorated in soft earth tones energized with flashes of red: a ceramic vase on the fireplace mantel, a few strategically placed pillows on the off-white sectional, a cluster of amaryllis rising from a crystal bowl on the coffee table. A ten-foot Christmas tree decorated with red garland and white lights stood in the corner near the fireplace.

"We didn't put up a tree this year…" I said, "…with the move and all."

"This might be the last one for me," she said. With sad brown eyes that were absent their normal sparkle, she gazed at the tree and added, "It all seems pretty pointless now."

I guessed that she must be on some type of antidepressant. During a brief fling with Xanax, which my doctor assured me would enable me to walk alone into a roomful of strangers without throwing up, Terry kept asking me what was wrong with my eyes. I was so zombie-like back then that I never thought to look in the mirror. Now I knew what he'd meant.

In the kitchen, I set the food on the counter. "When is the last time you had something to eat?"

"This morning. I had some toast."

Now that I was here, I had no idea how to broach the subject of Nathan's death. I had to say something and get it behind me. The only thing I could come up with was the truth. "I don't know what to say to make it better."

"There's nothing anyone can say to make this better."

I fixed a plate and placed it in front of her.

"I found a bottle of Chianti in the wine pantry," she said. She filled two delicately stemmed glasses. "Aren't you eating?"

"I had dinner with Terry and…" I was actually afraid to say Jeff's name aloud for fear of reminding her that it belonged to a living, breathing young man, while her son's name would forever be attached to a memory. My uncompleted sentence seemed to have escaped her notice, so I just left it hanging there.

We perched on stools at a granite-topped island that was larger than my dining room table.

"Can you believe it…they took his bike." She took a long drink of the wine. "Do you think it's possible that someone killed Nate over a lousy bike?"

I started to say something about Nathan's supposed meeting with Hunter, but clamped my lips shut just in time. "Anything's possible these days. What do the police say?"

"Nothing, yet. Someone from the Tempe Police Department, a Detective Staatz, is stopping by tomorrow morning."

"We've met." She looked at me, her silence a question mark. "Jeff was at our place yesterday, and Detective Staatz came over to ask him some questions." I tried to keep my tone casual to deflect any resentment Dinah might have about my son—the son whom the angels had seen fit to deliver from evil.

"Would you be willing to come over tomorrow when he's here? I—I could use the extra support. My parents will be coming up from Tucson for the funeral, but they won't be here till tomorrow afternoon."

"Of course…just tell me when."

For nearly half an hour, I watched Dinah use her fork to push pieces of lasagna around on a plate. I think the fork made it to her mouth a few times, but I'm not totally positive if the food ever actually reached its destination. She poured another glass of wine, and I asked her if she should be drinking alcohol with whatever medication she was taking. Her response was a shrug. I called Terry, and 15 minutes later he pulled into the drive.

I gave Dinah a final hug. "I'll see you tomorrow morning. Call me later if you want…anytime."

For Dinah's sake, I was trying to be reassuring and positive, but a stark hopelessness, so thick and oppressive that it covered me like a veil, followed me home that night.

Chapter Seven
Monday

Since Terry had to leave for work at eight a.m., Jeff gave me a ride to Dinah's house at nine.

"Do you want to come in and say hi?" I asked.

"No thanks. I've got a class."

Wondering whether avoidant behavior was a genetic mutation, I waved him off with an air kiss and watched until his orange RAV4 disappeared around the corner. Dinah opened the door before I had a chance to ring the bell. She'd set up a tray of sweet rolls and coffee in the living room.

"The neighbors have been bringing food over like there's no tomorrow. I'd much rather share it than throw it out."

I went into the kitchen for cream and sugar and noticed that she'd left the pan of lasagna out on the counter overnight. I scraped the leftovers into the drain, turned on the garbage disposal, and washed the pan.

When I returned to the living room, I was surprised to see that Detective Staatz had arrived. Dinah must have been watching for him the same way she'd been watching for me, because I hadn't heard the doorbell. His eyes, squinting against the late morning light streaming in through the lead-paned windows, widened when he saw me. "Mrs. Winters," he nodded, and sat in a chair across from the sectional, where I took a seat next to Dinah.

"I asked Amanda to join us," said Dinah. "I hope that was all right."

"Of course…whatever makes you comfortable." He helped himself to a cup of coffee and turned on his iPad. "Mrs. Reynolds, I have to ask you some questions about your husband."

Dinah frowned. "Why? Tom has nothing to do with this."

"When is the last time you spoke to him?"

"I haven't heard from him in ten years. I have no idea where he's living now."

"Did you know that your son found a metal box containing some of your husband's papers…notes from the case he was working on and email printouts related to that case? There was also a ten-year-old calendar page from the day your husband left: April 18."

Dinah's eyes sharpened for a moment. "No, I didn't know that Nate had any of his father's things." She shook her head as if to rouse herself from a dream. "I thought Tom had taken everything with him when he left…everything to do with his law practice, I mean. He left all his personal things behind. Clothes, books…he didn't even take a picture of Nate with him." Her voice deepened with resentment. "He took the Triumph, of course. That's the one thing he would never leave behind."

Staatz looked up with interest. "The Triumph? What year was it?"

"Seventy-five. He'd been searching for years, and finally found one in mint condition, royal blue. He paid quite a bit to have it brought here…had it shipped from Connecticut."

Staatz was silent for several minutes while he made notes. The man was thorough.

Finally, he looked up from his pad. "Do you know a man named Anthony Hunter?"

"I don't think so." Dinah leaned forward, her gaze clouded but nevertheless intense. "Is he the man who killed my son?"

"For now, he's a person of interest. I'll be heading over to talk to him after we're done here." He glanced down at his notes. "Over the phone, he told me he was tied up in a poker game Friday night. I'll be confirming that."

"Hunter sent some threatening emails to Tom just before he disappeared—the ones in the box," I explained. The words were still resonating when I realized I never should have said them.

Dinah turned to me. "What are you talking about? I didn't know about any emails…"

I shifted uncomfortably and looked to Staatz for help, but none was forthcoming. I wanted to keep Jeff out of this as much as possible, but I had to come clean if my explanation was to make any sense. "Jeff found Tom's box at the apartment yesterday…in his aquarium. Nathan told Jeff that he'd found it in your garage last week. For some reason, he thought that whatever was in it was worth hiding."

"Just before he left, did your husband mention that he'd been receiving threats?" Staatz asked.

I was relieved when Dinah shifted her focus back to the detective. "No. But he always made it a point to keep our family life and his work separate. I still don't see what any of this has to do with my son's death."

"On the night he was murdered, Nathan planned to meet with someone who had an appointment with your husband ten years ago, on April 18. It may or may not have been Anthony Hunter."

Dinah's voice quavered. "I…I still don't understand."

"A decade ago, Hunter was a leader in the tribal environmentalist movement. Pima activists launched a campaign to protest what they claimed was 'irresponsible spraying of pesticides' by some of the area's big cotton farmers." Staatz paused and directed a pointed look at Dinah. "Does any of this ring a bell?"

She shook her head. "I remember that there were some protests back then, but Tom never mentioned that they were connected to one of his cases."

"According to your husband's case notes, one of his clients was Dieter Imfeldt, a main target of Hunter's group. Hunter accused Imfeldt of spraying his cotton fields with DDT. He insisted the poison had gotten into the reservation's food and water supply, making a lot of people sick, including his own wife."

"But wasn't DDT banned years ago?" asked Dinah.

"Yeah, but, unfortunately, that didn't stop a number of farmers in the area from using it," said Staatz.

"Why would Hunter blame Tom for something one of his clients did?" I asked. "I mean, even if Imfeldt was using DDT, how would Tom have known?"

"He most likely wouldn't have." Staatz turned toward Dinah. "My guess is that Hunter saw your husband as an accomplice because he represented Imfeldt in the tribal hearings."

Dinah's voice had lost what little strength it had when we'd started the conversation. "The last few weeks before he left, Tom was so preoccupied that, at times, it seemed as if Nate and I were invisible to him. There were nights he never came to bed." She stared at her hands, which were folded tightly in her lap. "I— thought he was having an affair. It must have been those hearings, the emails…"

"But you never discussed them?"

She shook her head. "Tom made a point of not discussing his cases with me." She stood and walked to the Christmas tree, removed an ornament, and immediately replaced it in the exact same spot. "You're saying that Nate met with this Hunter and was murdered because he asked him about the emails he sent to Tom ten years ago?"

"I'm not saying anything at this point. We don't know for sure that Nathan met with Hunter...we don't even know if he actually met with anyone. Your husband also had appointments on the eighteenth to meet with Imfeldt and another client named Richard May, a business associate of Imfeldt's."

I waited for Staatz to bring up the possibility that Tom had also been murdered, but he didn't.

"Have you talked to them?" asked Dinah.

"May died in a car accident shortly before your husband left. I'm trying to set something up with Imfeldt, but he's 83 now, and not in the best of health. His business is pretty much handled by his board of directors these days." Staatz tapped off his iPad and stood. "I'll also be talking to Nathan's girlfriend, Danielle Palmer." He glanced at Dinah, and his voice bore a trace of discomfort when he asked the next question. "Mrs. Reynolds, when did you last speak to Nathan?"

"I phoned him late in the afternoon on New Year's Day." Dinah closed her eyes. "He and Danielle had gone to a New Year's Eve block party...Nate said they had an 'amazing time.'" When she opened her eyes again, they were flooded with tears.

Like a yawn that jumps from one person to another, her tears prompted mine to start up.

"The day after Christmas, I flew to Vegas," said Dinah. "It's an annual thing for realtors, a sort of combination business meeting and New Year's celebration. I should have come home right away—I never should have stayed for that party."

Staatz put a tentative hand on Dinah's shoulder. "There was nothing you could have done to prevent what happened." He noticed me watching him and quickly stepped back into his detached, professional mien. "I want you to know that I'm opening an official investigation into your husband's disappearance. We have to rule out any connection to your son's case."

Dinah's face strained with a sudden realization. "I do remember something Tom told me. One of his colleagues, Steven Bryce, became very angry when one of the firm's big accounts was taken away from him and given to Tom—that was a few months before he left. I don't know if the account was Dieter Imfeldt, though."

"Do you remember anything else about that…about Bryce?"

"Only that, at the time, Bryce made a big scene about it in the office." The hint of a memory played on her face. "Tom called it a tantrum." Clearly disturbed by the recollection, she rubbed her arms anxiously. "Do you think it's possible that Tom was murdered?"

"Anything's possible," said Staatz. "A data search failed to find so much as a driver's license currently issued to your husband, though he may be living under an assumed name. And any evidence of a crime, if one occurred, might be hard to come by ten years after the fact. Right now, all we have to go on are those emails and a calendar that may or may not include the names of everyone your husband met with on the last day you saw him."

"Ten years is a long time," I said. "Isn't there a statute of limitations?"

"No, ma'am…not for murder."

"Will you let me know what you find?" asked Dinah.

"Of course." He handed her a business card. "I'll be following up with Steven Bryce. If you can think of anything, anything at all, that might be relevant, please call me." He stopped and turned on the front path. "I want to stress this: Any connection between Nathan's murder and your husband's disappearance is pure conjecture at this point. We haven't yet ruled out robbery as a motive for Nathan's murder: His bike, cell phone, and laptop have yet to be recovered."

After closing the door, Dinah, without so much as a glance in my direction, carried the tray into the kitchen. Like a puppy that's just been caught piddling on the floor, I cowered at her heels.

"Please don't be angry," I said. "I didn't think you could handle the notes and the emails, what with Nathan's funeral and everything else."

She spun to face me, so violently that I thought for a moment she was going to slap me. "I'll be the one to decide what I can or can't handle. Whatever was in that box belonged to Tom and might relate directly to Nate's murder. Those notes and emails might even be able to help me understand why Tom left us without so much as a word. You had no right to keep them from me." She pulled open the dishwasher door with so much force that it bounced back on its hinges with a protesting groan.

"I'm sorry, Dinah."

Using Dinah's landline to call Aunt Sally, I asked her to pick me up, recovered my lasagna pan from the counter, and slipped out the front door to wait at the curb.

*****

At home, after a few hours of editing, I gave in to curiosity and Googled "Anthony Hunter." Several articles from Phoenix area newspapers confirmed that, ten years ago, Hunter had been a powerful activist leader in opposition to crop dusting and any kind of pesticide use on or near the Gila River Indian Reservation.

The Pima environmentalists claimed that the pesticides were contaminating drinking water and food crops, while the cotton growers insisted that even small amounts of rainfall leached the pesticides and defoliants from the soil, rendering the chemicals harmless. Several hearings were held by the tribal government that delved into the spraying practices of the area's cotton growers, including Dieter Imfeldt.

I also found an obituary and a brief article about Hunter's wife, Evelyn, who had succumbed to cancer ten years ago, two months before Tom had vanished. There was a family photo of Evelyn with her husband and 16-year-old son, Aaron. Aaron would be 26 now.

If Nathan had managed to connect with Anthony Hunter and set up a meeting with him, it would be reasonable to assume that Anthony mentioned it to his son: If Hunter's poker-game alibi was solid, it would be logical for Staatz to take a look at Aaron. It wouldn't be the first time the "sins of the father" had been taken up—and carried to the next level—by the son.

A mother's painful, lingering death would have left scars, especially in a teenage boy. Would those scars, I wondered, be deep enough to compel him, a decade later, to seek vengeance by going after the son of one of his mother's perceived murderers?

Chapter Eight
Thursday

Terry and I picked up Aunt Sally on the way to Nathan's funeral. "Arnold's in the shop," she said. "The gas over at the K-Corral didn't agree with him."

Jeff insisted on taking his own car. We met him at the church's main entrance and exchanged a few somber pleasantries. In the narthex, we waited in line to sign the guest book before walking into the sanctuary.

Dinah sat in the first pew directly in front of the closed coffin. With vacant eyes, she stared up at a large wooden sculpture of Jesus, whose hands were raised as if to bless the congregation. I knew without a doubt that she was in the process of bargaining: *Please, I'm begging you...turn back the clock, undo this horrible thing that has been done, and I will do anything, give you anything...*

I started up the aisle toward her, but Terry caught my sleeve and pulled me into one of the center pews. "Let's just wait," he said in a low whisper.

A steady stream of young men and women, many of them wearing ASU jackets, went up to pay their last respects. An abundant spray of yellow roses, baby's breath, and ivy rested atop the casket, surrounded by smaller arrangements that were mostly done in the Sun Devils' colors of maroon and gold. A plush Sparky, the team mascot, sat at the foot of the casket. The arrangement of calla lilies I'd ordered, decorated with a "Beloved Godson" banner, had been placed on a stand in front of the coffin. On a card table covered in white linen, a digital photo album flashed a collage of highlights from Nathan's short life. Jeff appeared in many of the pictures. One in particular brought back memories that set my heart to aching: Jeff sitting next to Nathan at one of their many shared birthday parties. It had been taken at Organ Piper Pizza: Both boys were grinning, and their arms were slung over each other's shoulders. With their hair too long and their teeth a bit too large for their mouths, they'd turned eleven that day…on the verge of discovering organized sports, rap music, and girls.

I had to look away, anywhere but at those photos, and in the pew parallel to ours, spotted a girl sitting with a man of about 45. I noticed her because she was movie-star pretty: flawless skin, dark eyes that didn't need liner or mascara, and auburn hair that fell in loose curls to her shoulders. Her head was down, her chin nearly resting on her chest.

From my side of the aisle, I could see tears fall from her eyes and into her lap; they were coming too quickly to simply roll down her cheeks. I nudged Jeff. "Is that Danielle?" He leaned forward in the pew, looked, and nodded.

Strains of "What a Friend We Have in Jesus," began to flow from the organ loft, and Pastor Mike approached the lectern behind and to the right of Nathan's coffin. During a reading of the 23rd Psalm, I peeked over to take another look at Danielle. Her weeping had moderated some, no thanks, I thought, to the man sitting next to her, whom I assumed was her father, Marty Palmer. He sat stiffly in the pew, his arms folded across his chest, and stared with disinterest at a stained glass depiction of the Last Supper on the window to his right. I sneaked a look over my shoulder and saw Detective Staatz standing just outside the entryway to the sanctuary. He was observing the funeral attendees and making copious notes on his iPad.

Dinah's parents, Carolyn and Frank Reade, were seated in the front pew with their daughter. She sat between them, her head resting on her father's ample shoulder. Though I couldn't hear her weeping, I could see her slight frame trembling violently from the force of her sobs. My heart went out to her as I mourned her loss and what she still would have to face at the cemetery.

Since the burial was to be private, refreshments were served in the fellowship hall after the short service, thereby giving friends an opportunity to mingle and share memories of Nathan. I looked around for Detective Staatz, but he'd apparently decided that the gathering wouldn't be worth his while…or maybe he harbored some sort of social phobia: Believe it or not, the feminine gender isn't the only one prone to chronic, irrational fears.

"Would you introduce me to Danielle?" I asked Jeff. "I'd like to meet her."

I left Terry to mind Aunt Sally, and we started across the room to where Danielle and her father sat at a long table. Halfway across the room, everything began to spin, the people and objects around me jumping in and out of focus before fading into a wavering blanket of fog. This was troubling. Normally, the presence of a trusted someone—Terry, Jeff, or Dinah, in particular— kept my panic attacks at bay. I closed my eyes, took a deep breath, then continued to the table and fell heavily into the chair across from Danielle.

She regarded me with a mixture of concern and annoyance. Her face relaxed into a smile when she realized I was with Jeff. "Hey."

"I just wanted to come over and see how you're doing," he said. "This is my mom."

Danielle reached across the table and offered her hand. "I'm Danielle."

I paused for a moment, relieved that my breathing had nearly returned to normal and that the room was standing still again. Baby attacks, I called these episodes, which seemed to take great pleasure in tormenting me with short, intense blasts. "I'm Amanda," I said, accepting her hand. "Nathan talked about you a lot. Nice things…you know?"

"I loved him very much," she said, her voice faltering.

My gaze fell to her wrist and to an expensive-looking silver braid set with onyx stones. "What a lovely bracelet."

"Dad bought it for my mom in Mexico years ago." She glanced self-consciously at the man sitting next to her. "She thought I should have it, so she gave it to me for Christmas."

Jeff and I waited for Marty Palmer to take a breather from his doughnut long enough to acknowledge our presence. When he failed to do so, Danielle touched his arm and said, "Dad, Jeff was Nate's roommate. They grew up together."

"Hi, Mr. Palmer," said Jeff.

I offered my hand in greeting; Palmer looked at it, then to the cruller in his own, and back to my hand again. The cruller won.

"Nice to meet you," I said.

"Same here. It's unfortunate that we couldn't have met under happier circumstances."

"Jeff tells me you're on the faculty at ASU Polytechnic. We toured the campus last year—it's beautiful."

"Yes, it is." He took another bite and brushed crumbs from his tie.

"Dad teaches aeronautics there," said Danielle, her voice reflecting more than a trace of pride.

Palmer's glance toward his daughter was brief but castigating. "It's aeronautic management technology, actually."

"Cool," said Jeff.

"Had you known Nathan long?" I asked Palmer.

"Unfortunately, I never got the chance to meet him."

"He was quite an amazing young man."

"So I've heard. Danielle's mother would have come instead, but she couldn't get the time off from work." He took a bite of his doughnut and added, "I'm afraid I don't do well at these things."

I felt a hand on my shoulder. "This might be a good time to say a few words to Dinah before they leave for the cemetery," said Terry.

I introduced Terry to Danielle and to Marty Palmer, and we engaged in small talk for a few minutes before excusing ourselves to find Dinah.

But she was nowhere to be found. Mr. and Mrs. Reade were speaking with Pastor Mike, and I interrupted to ask if they knew where their daughter was.

Carolyn Reade gave her husband a worried glance. "Dinah's waiting for us in the car," she said. "She's not doing very well...you can imagine..."

My stomach sank. "Of course. Tell her I'll be in touch soon."

We found Aunt Sally standing outside the front door of the church. She'd wrapped several sweet rolls in a paper napkin and was attempting to cram the bundle into her purse. "I love these cheese Danishes."

"Aunt Sally, really?!" I said, my eyes taking in the nearby clusters of people to see if anyone had noticed my aunt's indiscretion.

"What?!" she said. "It's not like they can hold them over for the next funeral. Pastor Mike will only take them home, and his robe is already too tight."

In the parking lot behind the church, a young man, his hands thrust into the pockets of a brown leather bomber jacket, stood alone to watch black-suited men from the funeral home load Nathan's casket into a waiting hearse. The man's jet black hair was pulled into a thick braid that trailed down his back, almost to his waist. I hadn't noticed him inside the church.

I was curious to know who he was, but I couldn't ask Jeff, who had taken off in another direction and was already starting up his car. When we walked past the man on our way to the Cruiser, I studied his face with increasing recognition. This man was Aaron Hunter, Anthony Hunter's son. I was sure of it. The online photo I'd seen had been taken ten years earlier, but the shape of the face was the same, the features were the same...a little rougher from a decade's worth of wear and tear. The boyish gleam in his dark eyes had been replaced by a hardness that seemed incongruous in someone under thirty.

I lagged behind Terry and Aunt Sally, and as I passed him I said, "Aaron?"

He turned to regard me with curiosity, but said nothing.

"You're Anthony's son, aren't you? Aaron?"

"You know my father?" His voice was deep and mellow...a singer's voice, I thought.

"Not exactly," I said, drawing out the words to give me some time to think of what I would say next.

Frank Reade pulled his sedan to a stop just behind the hearse and acknowledged me with a nod. Dinah, her head bowed low, was sitting in the backseat.

"Can we talk?" I put a hand on Aaron's arm and steered him well away from the hearse...and out of Dinah's direct line of vision.

His look changed from one of curiosity to distrust. "Are you a cop?"

"I was Nathan's godmother."

"Oh…sorry."

I acknowledged his sentiment with a nod. "I'm surprised to see you here."

The dark eyes fixed on mine. "My father sent me to pay our family's respects. He would have come himself, but he knew he wouldn't be welcome."

"No one's ever mistaken me for a cop before. Do I really look like one?" My voice was lighter—and braver—than I felt at the moment. We watched as the hearse, followed by the Reades' car, slowly pulled out of the lot and turned right toward Good Shepherd Cemetery. I shivered and I regretted having left my coat in the car. I crossed my arms in front of me and hugged them to my body for warmth.

My question had been hypothetical, but Aaron chose to answer it. "You know my father, you seem to know me, but we've never met. And you want to talk to me—not about the weather, I'm thinking."

"People I love are hurting, and I want to help them. It's that simple." I watched with curiosity as Jeff waited for Danielle and her father to get into Palmer's Silverado before following them out of the lot. "Nathan's murder makes absolutely no sense."

"And you think you're the one to make sense of it?"

"No, but even when something doesn't make sense, there has to be a reason behind it. Cause and effect; it's a rule of nature."

"Did you know that the cops always stake out the funerals of murder victims in case the killer decides to show up?"

"So I've heard."

He nodded. "I met Staatz, the Tempe PD dude with the long hair, yesterday. He was here earlier. He could be part Pima."

I managed a smile. "You may be right." I drew my arms in even more closely to my body, cupping my elbows with my hands, and shifted on my feet a bit. I watched Aaron's face carefully for a reaction to my next statement. "Your father's been named as a person of interest in Nathan's murder."

"Yeah, well, that's a problem. The only connection my father had to Nathan Reynolds was a friendship with his father ten years ago."

"Friendship? That's an interesting term for it. Who sends their friends threatening emails?"

"My father regrets sending those emails. Like he told Staatz, he and Reynolds made peace with each other before Reynolds disappeared." His jaw muscles tensed, and his eyes grew even darker. "You seem to know a lot for someone who's not a cop."

"Nathan discovered the emails in his mother's garage. My son Jeff found them hidden in the apartment they shared."

"So what's that supposed to prove?"

"Nothing, really," I admitted. "The boys' apartment was ransacked a few days ago—I thought that maybe your father might have been looking to get his emails back. Anyway, Detective Staatz has them now."

I turned to see Terry hurrying across the parking lot to where I stood with Aaron. From several yards away, I could see the concern on his face. His expression turned to alarm when I introduced him to Hunter, who nevertheless offered a handshake.

"Aaron was just telling me about his father," I said. "Did you know that his father Anthony was a friend of Tom's?"

Terry played along. "No, I did not know that."

Aaron turned to watch the hearse as it slowly pulled out of the lot. "My father tried to tell the cops ten years ago that Tom Reynolds didn't run away...that someone got rid of him, but no one would listen." He shook his head in bewilderment. "Now they've opened an investigation into his murder after his son turns up dead—too little too late, if you ask me."

I started to respond when Aaron's cell phone rang. He listened for a few minutes and said numbly, "No." All color had begun to drain from his face.

"Is something wrong?" I asked.

He pocketed the phone and said, his voice breaking, "My father's been arrested. They found Nathan Reynolds' bike in the woods behind his house."

Chapter Nine

Terry and I watched as Aaron Hunter climbed into his truck, a mud-spattered Dodge Ram, and tore out of the parking lot.

"That was fast work," I said.

"Do me a favor and don't say anything to anyone about Hunter's arrest," said Terry.

"Oh, believe me, I learned my lesson after letting it slip about those emails in front of Dinah. I'll let Detective Staatz take care of all case updates from now on."

Hand in hand, we headed for the Cruiser, where Aunt Sally was waiting in the backseat. Before we'd gotten halfway to the car, Pastor Mike, his robe open and billowing around him like the cape of an angelic superhero, came running across the parking lot toward us. He held a large pot containing a towering bird of paradise plant.

"Amanda! Terry! Wait!"

He caught up to us and bent slightly forward while he tried to catch his breath. "Whew! I didn't think I'd catch you in time."

"In time for what?" I asked.

He held the bird of paradise plant in front of him and peeked through the tall green spikes at us. "Will you do me the favor of taking this over to Dinah's house tonight? She left it behind. I'd do it myself, but I've got a counseling session at seven."

"Can't you give it to her at the cemetery?" I asked. Rather than provide Dinah another opportunity to attack me for keeping Hunter's emails from her, I thought it might be a good idea to give her wide berth for a few days. I knew that eventually she'd come to the realization that I'd acted in her best interest. She wouldn't have brought up the incident at the church in front of her family, but I suspected she'd have no trouble continuing the tongue-lashing in private, on her own turf.

"The funeral home is handling the burial," said Pastor Mike. His expression was crestfallen as he added, "I was told that I won't be needed at the cemetery."

"I have to head into the station for a production meeting," said Terry, checking his watch. "I won't be home till after nine. We could head over to Dinah's after that, but it might be better to wait until tomorrow."

Aunt Sally poked her head out the window of the Cruiser. "If you take me over to pick up Arnold at the K-Corral, I can drive Amanda to Dinah's. I don't have anything else to do tonight. All my shows are still in holiday reruns."

*****

Terry transferred the bird of paradise to Arnold's back floor before leaving for the station. Since my kitchen still wasn't in any shape for cooking a proper meal, I'd invited Aunt Sally and Jeff to dinner at a neighborhood sports bar. I was hoping that the myriad of TVs broadcasting every type of sport imaginable would help to raise Jeff's mood, at least for a little while. He told us that he'd gone out to the Phoenix-Mesa Gateway Airport with Danielle and her father after the funeral to check out the planes. "He's a real nice guy. He's teaching Danielle how to fly, and he offered to give me a free lesson, just to see if it was something I might be interested in."

"Wonderful," I said, with no small degree of sarcasm. Aviophobia, the fear of flying, is a kissing cousin of agoraphobia, so the very idea of getting into an airplane starts my stomach to churning. People mistakenly believe that agoraphobia is a fear of open spaces, but it's actually the fear of losing control. Since flying in an airplane would be ceding control to some pilot who may have had four hours of sleep and five martinis before take-off, our vacations are restricted to less-than-exotic places within driving distance. And cruises are out, since I also suffer from hydrophobia, the fear of water. Now that we've inherited a pool, Terry is determined to put that one to rest sooner rather than later.

We said our good-byes to Jeff at the restaurant. As Aunt Sally pulled up to the curb in front of Dinah's house, I gave serious consideration as to whether I should let her handle the flower delivery on her own while I stayed with Arnold. I decided against it for two reasons: one, if Dinah wanted to vent her anger, I'd swallow my pride and accommodate her need to do so—if the situation were reversed, I knew, she'd have done the same for me; and two, I doubted that Aunt Sally's five-foot-two, 120-pound frame could support the weight and bulk of the plant. I swung open the back door and lifted the pot from the floor only to poke myself in the eye with one of the sharp, pointed leaves, which prompted me to let loose with an uncharacteristic vulgarity.

Aunt Sally gave a little snort. "Glad to hear you're human, Amanda."

"Let's just get this thing delivered and be on our way."

We walked up the path to the front door and rang the bell. After a few minutes of waiting, I set the plant down and used the brass doorknocker. "Maybe the bell's not working."

"You better get your ears checked. I heard it plain and clear, and I'm a heck of a lot older than you." Aunt Sally craned her neck to get a good view through the side window. "The blinds are open a little, but I don't see much light in there. And no one's moving around."

From around the side of the house, we heard the loud clang of metal striking metal, followed by a crash. I'd once heard the same sound when a rambunctious little boy pushed over a pyramid of soup cans in the supermarket.

"I hope to heck you heard *that* racket. Someone's in the garage." Aunt Sally, her purse dangling from her forearm, made a beeline across the driveway and toward the sound.

"Wait," I whispered. "The light isn't on."

"Well, someone's in there poking around in the dark. And by the sound of it, they're making a real mess of things."

I stepped in front of her and turned the knob. The door was ajar, and its hinges creaked loudly when I pushed it open wide. When the door hit the garage wall with a bang, Aunt Sally gasped and moved more closely behind me.

"Dinah? Are you in here?" I reached inside and felt around for a light switch, but the only thing my hand came into contact with was something that felt like some sort of netting...at least I hoped it was some sort of netting. In a far corner, I spotted a small halo of light that had been directed at the wall and then abruptly disappeared. Someone had just clicked off a flashlight.

Aunt Sally grabbed a handful of my shirt and tugged. "Why would Dinah be fumbling around in the dark inside her own garage?" she whispered. "And why wouldn't she have answered you?"

"Good point," I whispered. I backed out through the door, nudging Aunt Sally along behind me. "Who's there?!" I demanded. "You'd better come out right now...we've already called 9-1-1!"

A tall figure dressed in black erupted from the doorway. He caught my left shoulder and knocked me off-balance, sending both me and Aunt Sally reeling backward and into a huge oleander. As I struggled to disentangle myself from a snarl of branches in the midst of the shrub, I tried in vain to get a good look at the man as he ran down the driveway and out to the street.

"Are you all right?!" I shifted my weight from where I'd landed squarely on my pint-sized aunt, and felt something cave in underneath me. "What was that?! Is something broken?!"

"Only the cheese Danishes. You're sitting on my purse."

I helped Aunt Sally to her feet. "I guess it could have been worse," I said.

"You got that right. The guy could have pushed us into one of those prickly pears."

The Reades' sedan pulled into the drive just then. Dinah and her parents, their eyes wide with concern, emerged from the car and hurried toward us.

Dinah's gaze took in our disheveled appearance and the crushed oleander behind us. "What are you doing back here? What happened?"

"We came to deliver a plant you forgot at the church," I said, "and ran into a prowler inside your garage."

"Actually, it was the other way around," said Aunt Sally. "He ran into us."

"I always keep the garage locked." Dinah walked over to the door and examined the lock. "Someone pried this open. The wood along the edge is chipped away." She closed the door as best she could. "Who would do this? Especially today..."

I had a sudden vision of Nathan's casket being lowered into the ground, separating Dinah from her son with a finality that I couldn't even begin to comprehend. I shook off the vision before it had a chance to ignite an emotional blitzkrieg inside my head.

"We didn't get a good look at him," I said. "It's pretty dark back here. The garage door light must be burned out."

Frank Reade reached up to check the bulb, and light flooded the door and the patch of driveway outside it. "Someone must have unscrewed the bulb."

"I didn't see a face," said Aunt Sally, "but I saw the back of the guy. He looked like one of those Mill Avenue hippies—you know—the ones with hair practically down to their behinds."

Aaron Hunter matched that description, I thought. And earlier that day outside the church, I'd mentioned to Aaron that Nathan had found Anthony Hunter's emails in the garage. But I'd also made it clear that the emails were now in Staatz's possession. If the intruder had indeed been Aaron, and he hadn't been looking for the emails, then what, I wondered, *had* he been looking for?

Chapter Ten

I urged Dinah to call Detective Staatz's direct number to report the break-in.

"But he's with Homicide. Why would I call him for a break-in? Besides, Staatz is with the Tempe force…he has no jurisdiction in Chandler."

"It's strange that someone broke into your garage today, right after I—" I was about to say, "right after I mentioned to Aaron Hunter that Nathan found his father's emails in the garage," but I cut my words off mid-sentence, something I'd been doing a lot lately. "I just think he'd want to know."

"He's already arrested Anthony Hunter. Don't you think he'll be closing out Nate's case?"

"I suspect that the only thing tying this break-in to Nathan's case," said Frank Reade, "is that some crook scanned the obituaries and was hoping to help himself to some power tools while we were attending Nathan's funeral."

"Maybe so," I ceded, "but I'd still give Staatz a call—out of courtesy, if for no other reason." I wanted to remind Dinah that the detective had opened a second case, an investigation into Tom's disappearance, but that would also remind her about the emails, which might stoke her anger again. I felt that, as far as Dinah was concerned, a little eggshell-walking couldn't hurt, at least for the foreseeable future. After what she'd been through this week, I'd walk barefoot over hot coals if I thought it would help her.

"I'll give Detective Staatz a call and see what he says," said Mr. Reade. He took his daughter's hand and said, "And you…I want you to try and relax a little."

After telling her I'd planned to wait with the others for Staatz to show up, Aunt Sally, still shaken from our encounter with the oleander but having sustained only a few scratches and no bruises that I could see, asked if I could catch a ride home with the Reades. "I want to get Arnold back to his garage, where he'll be safe from no-good hippie thieves."

"You got a look at the man, and I didn't," I said. "Detective Staatz will want to talk to you."

"Just give him my address. He'll find me at home in front of the TV, reruns or not, enjoying a nip of brandy." She gave me a conspiratorial wink. "Strictly medicinal, of course…steadies the nerves."

The rest of us went inside. Carolyn Reade disappeared into the kitchen to make coffee while Dinah, her father, and I settled in the living room.

When Staatz arrived, I told him that Aunt Sally and I had come to deliver the bird of paradise and heard noise from the garage. "That's about it," I said. "We went to investigate, and someone came crashing through the door and knocked us into the oleander. I didn't see him, but my Aunt Sally says she got a look at him, at least the back of him."

He looked around and asked, "Where's your aunt now?"

"Home," I said. "I told her you'd want to talk to her." I considered advising him to wait until tomorrow afternoon before visiting Aunt Sally, just to allow some time for the effects of that "nip of brandy" to wear off. I decided not to. After all, Staatz was a seasoned cop; I'm sure he'd encountered much worse than a tipsy 72-year-old woman.

"What's her address?" he asked. "I'll need to ask her some questions, see if I can get a description of your attacker."

"Do you have a pen?" I asked.

He pulled out the ubiquitous iPad. "Just give me the address."

I did so, and Dinah asked, "Why do you think he broke into the garage instead of the house? Wouldn't it have been just as easy to get in through the patio doors? I don't have an alarm system."

"First, I strongly suggest that you get one installed as soon as possible," said Staatz. "Second, the exterior of your house is pretty well lit. In the backyard, the intruder would have been exposed to neighbors on either side. If he'd tried to break in through the front door, he could easily have been seen by passing vehicles or by the neighbors across the street."

"But why the garage?" Dinah asked.

"It's set back from the street, and garages are popular targets. Since most of the homes in this area don't have attics or basements, people store all kinds of things there: tools, electronics, collectibles..." He turned to me. "Mrs. Winters, would you mind coming outside to show me exactly where you were and describe what happened?"

Grateful for the opportunity to talk to him alone, I led him outside to the garage. I was afraid that Dinah might choose to join us at any moment, so I poured my words out quickly and without the courtesy of providing context. "I talked to Aaron Hunter after the funeral today. I may have mentioned the fact that Nathan had found his father's emails in Dinah's garage."

"Whoa, there. How do you know Aaron Hunter?"

"I recognized him from a picture that ran in the paper with his mother's obituary."

He frowned in bemusement. "Really."

"I got curious and did a little Internet surfing." I cleared my throat and glanced nervously over my shoulder. I needed to get this out before Dinah decided to show up. "Anyway, when my Aunt Sally gives you her description of the intruder, you may notice that it bears a slight resemblance to Aaron Hunter."

Out came the iPad. "Consider this a warning, Mrs. Winters. Don't say anything to Aaron Hunter, or to anyone else, about what we've discussed concerning this case. In fact, stay away from Hunter altogether."

"I have no plans to do otherwise. But why the warning? You arrested his father, not him."

"I have my reasons." He examined the door and used his pad to take some photos. "And yes, I did arrest Anthony Hunter, but nothing's even near being cut-and-dried. I'm still waiting to hear back from the D.A. on whether there's enough evidence to charge him with murder."

"Anyway," I said, "I also mentioned to Aaron that we gave you the emails. So there really would be no reason for him to break into the garage. The intruder was probably a would-be thief, like you said."

"Maybe." He stepped into the garage, found the light switch, and flipped it on.

"I mean, crooks read the obituaries to find potential houses to break into, don't they? They know that relatives of the deceased will probably leave their houses empty the day of the funeral. At least, that's what Dinah's father thinks."

From the garage doorway, I studied Detective Staatz as he walked to the center of the room and moved in an increasing spiral to examine every detail of the large interior. I felt an admiration, strangely akin to pride, as I watched him at work. His technique was practiced and methodical.

"You enjoy what you do," I observed.

He paused to consider that for a moment. "I guess I do, now that you mention it." He made some notes in his iPad and asked, "What do you do for a living, Mrs. Winters?"

"Nothing as exciting as your job, I'm afraid. I freelance from home as a copy editor. I used to teach high school, but once my panic attacks started to scare the students, the school board 'strongly suggested' early retirement."

He looked up hopefully. "Did you teach math?"

"English."

His expression deflated. "Too bad...I have a nephew who could use some help with algebra."

"Sorry." I unfolded a lawn chair that had been propped against a wall, and sat down. "Can I ask you something?"

He shrugged. "Sure, but you might not get an answer." He cocked his head and peered at me over the top of his glasses. "And please don't touch anything else. This is a crime scene."

I jumped up from the lawn chair, refolded it, and, resisting an urge to wipe off my fingerprints, put it back where I'd found it. "Did your forensics team come away with anything from the boys' apartment?"

"Not a thing. Whoever trashed the place either wore gloves or wiped everything clean." He stared thoughtfully at the floor. "Forensics couldn't get prints from Nathan's bike, either. Funny that Hunter would take the time to wipe it down before stowing it in the woods behind his own backyard."

"Not to mention that one would think he'd have found a better hiding place," I said.

Staatz shrugged. "Most criminals aren't the sharpest tacks in the drawer."

"Knives," I said with a smile. "I think the phrase is 'sharpest knives in the drawer.'"

"Yeah...right."

"You still haven't found Nathan's laptop or phone?"

"No." He walked over to one of the shelves, removed a small box, and opened it. "Huh...rubber bands. Who saves rubber bands?"

"These days, probably no one. What about Anthony Hunter's alibi? Did the poker game thing pan out?"

"It did. But Hunter's community is tight-knit. People usually don't think twice about lying to the police to protect one of their own."

The garage door opened with a bang, causing both of us to jump.

"Dinah," I said, hoping my voice didn't betray my guilt. Had she overheard us carrying on yet another conversation about Nathan's death from which she was excluded? I hoped not. "I was just watching the detective at work. Fascinating."

"I'm going to have to do something about that door." She bent down to pick up one of the paint cans that had toppled from a shelf onto the concrete floor. "I don't see anything in here that could possibly be of interest to a thief." I noticed that she was weaving slightly.

Staatz noticed it, too. "You'd be surprised at what thieves find interesting." He moved over and took her gently by one shoulder to steady her. "Here, let me help with that." He picked up the can and set it next to the few that remained on a shelf near the workbench. His gaze remained focused on Dinah as he asked me the next question. "Mrs. Winters, did you notice if the perp was carrying anything?"

I had to smile. I'd never before heard the word *perp* outside of TV crime shows or the movies. "I don't think so...at least I didn't see anything."

Staatz clicked off his pad. "Mrs. Reynolds, I'd see about getting that lock replaced right away."

Dinah studied the door for a few seconds as if to remind herself of the damage that had been done to it. "The locksmith's coming first thing tomorrow."

"And that alarm system?"

"I'll make some calls."

"Good. In the meantime, I'm going to write up a report for the Chandler department and try and get a description of the intruder from Mrs. Winters' aunt."

At Staatz's car, Dinah surprised us by asking if she could meet with Anthony Hunter.

"Why would you want to do that?" he asked.

She shrugged. "I'm not sure, exactly. I only know that I have to talk to him."

Staatz scratched thoughtfully at a considerable five o'clock shadow while he considered the prospect. "Well, there's no law against it, although I don't see what possible good could come of it."

"I'll go with her," I blurted.

Dinah cast a look of annoyance at me and was about to protest when Staatz said, "That would work, I guess."

"Where do we go?" Dinah asked.

"He's at the jail on East 5th," said Staatz. "Not too far from my substation."

"We'll find it," I said. "Are there visiting hours we should know about?"

"Anytime between 6:30 a.m. and 2:30 p.m."

I walked Staatz to his car. I thought Dinah was right behind me, but she'd turned in the opposite direction and went into the house without a word. After seeing the detective off, I walked up to the front door and was somewhat relieved to find that she hadn't locked me out. Frank Reade rose from his chair when I entered the living room and asked if I was ready to go home.

We watched with concern as Dinah held the railing to steady her gait while ascending the stairs to her bedroom. "I'll pick you up at seven sharp, Amanda. Be ready." The words were shrill and slurred, tossed over her shoulder the same way a handful of salt is thrown by the superstitious to ward off the devil.

During the ride to Sun Lakes, Mr. Reade said, "You'll have to forgive my daughter. Her mother and I are worried about her, you know."

"I'm worried, too. And there's nothing to forgive. She just buried her son. In my opinion, she's doing quite well considering everything that's happened."

"Carolyn and I went with her to identify Nathan's body Tuesday morning." He sighed heavily. "That's something no mother should ever have to do. They use closed-circuit television now, but it was brutal. For a moment there, I thought we were going to lose her, too."

I pictured Nathan's face, gray and lifeless, his body prone on a cold mortuary slab. When the face morphed into Jeff's, I closed my eyes to erase the image and said. "She's strong. She'll get through this."

"I don't think Dinah should go to see Hunter."

"It might give her the closure she needs to move on. Anyway, I'll be with her."

"I could come with you…"

"Not necessary…she'll be fine," I promised.

That was a promise, however, that I would be unable to keep.

Chapter Eleven
Friday

At precisely seven a.m. the next morning, as promised, Dinah's silver Audi TTS Roadster pulled into our drive. She didn't honk the horn or get out of the car, but sat stiffly in the driver's seat and stared straight ahead at the garage door. A Sun Lakes garbage truck, its rumble loud enough to shake the front windows, barreled past the house but failed to elicit so much as a blink from her.

"Good morning," I said with feigned cheerfulness. I'd awakened this morning with some serious doubts about our dropping into the Tempe jail to chat with Anthony Hunter, but it was too late to back out now. And even if I did back out, I knew that Dinah wouldn't. At this point, the only course of action was to see this thing through and hope that the meeting would be a pivotal point for her.

Judging from the sickening sweet cloud of alcohol that permeated the car's interior, Dinah had poured herself something stronger than coffee for breakfast. If talking to Anthony Hunter didn't give her closure, as I'd suggested to her father, I'd have to come up with some other plan to convince her not to go down the self-destructive path she seemed to have chosen.

"Morning," she said and, her eyes riveted on the steering wheel, started the car.

"Dinah," I said. "We need to talk."

She pulled onto Riggs Road and headed for the freeway. "Talk away." She glanced in the rearview mirror and applied a heavy foot to the accelerator. The car lurched forward, sending my handbag sailing off my lap and onto the floor. Apparently she hadn't spotted any patrol cars in the mirror and decided that driving twenty miles over the 45-mile per hour speed limit would be a good idea. I recaptured my purse and the lipstick that had escaped its confines, leaving a handful of loose change where it had disappeared under the seat for some lucky kid to find during the Audi's next car wash.

"I lost both my parents this year, but I can't begin to imagine what it must be like to go through...what you're going through."

"No, Amanda, you can't."

"You're angry. I absolutely get that...scream your lungs out, throw something, smash something to pieces...but mixing pills and alcohol will only make it worse."

She turned to glare at me, and the car shuddered as its right tires hit the gravel shoulder of the road. "I want you to do something for me, Amanda. I want you to imagine that someone has just told you that Jeff has been murdered."

I didn't know how to respond to that, so I kept silent and stared through the window to focus on the mountains in the distance. That, however, was the wrong response: The speed of the car increased as Dinah's anger accelerated to culminate in a rage that distracted her to the point that she was unable to keep even an occasional eye on the road. The car swung to the left, and she overcompensated by turning the wheel too far to the right so that the car hit the shoulder again, this time with a jarring bounce. I glanced into the side mirror and prayed that I'd see flashing lights coming up behind us. I should have pulled Dinah from behind the wheel of the car while I still had the chance…while we were still alive.

"I mean it, Amanda!" she said. "Close your eyes and imagine it…you've just learned that your son is dead...you don't know how much he suffered before he died—how much pain there was—what his last thoughts were."

I closed my eyes and struggled to keep my tears in check. I was supposed to be the one in control here. "I…I can't."

"No, you can't. And a week ago, neither could I. So don't tell me what will make this worse, because believe me, honey, it doesn't get any worse than this."

"There are people who love you who want to help you through this—your parents, me…"

Tires squealed as she made a sharp right turn onto the entrance ramp to the I-10. "It's funny when the worst happens, Amanda. There's nothing left to be afraid of…even for people like you, people who act like raving lunatics every time the phone rings."

Her words had been carefully chosen to cause pain, and cause pain they did. I reminded myself that this wasn't really Dinah talking…it was the agony of a sorrow so unrelenting that it had her heart, mind, and soul firmly in its grasp. Dinah was a woman possessed.

I thought that I'd try to move her on to a more productive train of thought. I knew that Dinah would never be able to put Nathan's murder behind her, but maybe I'd been right when I'd told Frank Reade that this visit might be an opportunity for his daughter to put closure on one part of it. Maybe Dinah would be able to take some comfort in the fact that the man responsible for her son's death had already been apprehended and that there was a possibility he'd have to pay with his own life. In the state of Arizona, after all, the phrase "an eye for an eye" was still taken seriously.

"What do you plan to say to Hunter?" I asked.

"I don't know yet. But I'm sure something will come to mind."

"Your father doesn't think this meeting is a good idea. Maybe I don't either…is it too soon?"

She didn't answer, but continued down the interstate. I didn't push it. I'd read up on Kübler-Ross' stages of grief: denial, anger, bargaining, and depression. Dinah would have to work through the first four at her own pace before arriving at the final stage: acceptance. She'd get there eventually, but it was a transition that couldn't be forced or rushed.

I was relieved when we passed Sun Devil Stadium and got off at the 5th Street exit: Even if Dinah continued to speed, I figured that our chances of avoiding an accident would be better at 45 miles per hour than at 75. We parked in the side lot. I wanted to fall to my knees and kiss the pavement. Instead, I took Dinah's arm and said, "Are you ready for this?"

"I've never been more ready for anything in my life."

Slowly, we walked together up the front path. The building didn't look like a jail. It didn't look like much of anything, really: a nondescript red brick structure with bare-bones desert landscaping on the outside. Inside, we were greeted by a small reception area featuring a number of security cameras and a row of four kiosks with turnstiles. It was apparently too early in the day for other visitors. We were alone in the room with two guards, one who stood on our side of the turnstile, and one who stood on the other side.

The guard closest to us stepped forward as we approached. "Hold it right there."

"We're here to see Anthony Hunter," I said.

The guard offered no response.

"Detective Roy Staatz said it would be all right."

He nodded toward a small counter near the turnstile. "Take one of those trays and place all metal, cell phones, and weapons inside. You'll get everything back when you leave."

"Weapons?" I asked weakly. But of course, this was Arizona, where guns were as common as Rolexes in Beverly Hills.

I removed my watch and the belt from my jeans, and placed them in a plastic aqua tray. I asked if I could leave my wedding ring on, and the guard nodded with a roll of his eyes. Dinah followed my lead, and we walked through the turnstile, where the other guard scanned us with a wand. We signed in and were required to show our drivers' licenses before being given laminated visitor badges that had been hooked onto red elastic lanyards.

"Where is he?" Dinah asked the guard. Her voice sounded strangely hollow.

The second guard gestured toward a door with a small mesh-covered window. "Ring the bell, and Lyle, over there, will take you into the visiting area. Hunter's waiting for you."

Without so much as a nod, Dinah started toward the door.

"Thank you," I said to the guard with an apologetic smile.

By the time I'd caught up with Dinah, she'd already rung the bell. There was a loud, protracted buzzing, then a click as the lock was released and the door was opened. A short, chubby uniformed guard who walked with a pronounced waddle led us to a door on the opposite wall. He placed a hand on the steel bar and checked the wall clock. "You have thirty minutes," he said, and pushed down on the bar to open the door.

Separated from us by a glass wall reinforced with steel crosshatching, Anthony Hunter was seated in the exact center of a long wooden table lined with empty chairs. His hands rested awkwardly on the counter in front of him. His eyes watched us with a mix of curiosity and wariness as we entered the room and took seats at a table that mirrored his. I glanced at Dinah, who was studying him with eyes that could only be described as dead. She didn't say anything, but only sat there and stared at him: the man who she believed had taken from her the most precious thing in her life.

Hunter, dressed in a bright orange jumpsuit, bore a strong resemblance to his son, Aaron. He had the same broad face and strong features. His jawline and chin were unusually firm and strong for a man approaching sixty years, and I imagined that he'd been quite handsome back in the day. His hair, a steely gray, hung in two thin braids over his shoulders. He sat back in his chair and waited for one of us to make the first move. I studied

I studied Dinah from the corner of my eye, but could see no sign that she was ready to talk.

A line of telephones had been placed along the back edge of each counter, and I leaned forward in my chair and picked up the receiver from the one closest to me. Hunter took my cue and did the same.

"Mr. Hunter," I said into the receiver. "I'm Amanda Winters, Nathan's godmother." I nodded toward Dinah. "And this is Dinah Reynolds, Nathan's mother."

Hunter nodded into the receiver. If this was the way the meeting was headed, I would have to work out how to mediate solely by translating body language.

"Mrs. Reynolds requested this meeting," I said, and held the receiver out to Dinah.

To my surprise, she accepted it. "Mr. Hunter."

Hunter nodded.

"I understand that you're the one who murdered my son, and that it's quite possible that you also murdered my husband."

Hunter shook his head and spoke into the receiver, "No, I didn't."

"No, you didn't kill my son, or no, you didn't kill my husband?"

"I didn't kill anyone, Mrs. Reynolds. I never met your son, and your husband was my friend."

She emitted a dry laugh. "I heard all about your emails." She turned her head to glare at me. "Though I've never actually seen them." She turned away from me to face Hunter again. "Do you make it a habit to threaten your friends?"

Hunter stared down at his left hand, which was now drumming the tabletop nervously. "I apologized to your husband for sending those emails. He understood what I was going through…I'd just lost my wife to cancer. My mind wasn't right."

"My mind isn't quite right these days, either," said Dinah. "Your people believe in visions, don't they, Mr. Hunter? I've been having them…visions of how my son looked on the day he was born…when I got my first look at him. Visions of his lifeless body floating in the Salt River."

Hunter looked up, then, his eyes pleading and his gaze directed at me, as though he knew he wouldn't be able to get through to Dinah but that maybe he'd have a chance with me.

His voice was soft but insistent. "I saw Tom a few days before he disappeared. He told me he'd found evidence that would prove that Imfeldt was using DDT on his fields. He was going to bring that evidence to the hearings. He was going to help me…"

With her free hand, Dinah opened her handbag and withdrew a vial of pills. "You know what's been helping me, Mr. Hunter? These little pills right here. They help to numb the pain. Not all of it, of course…but enough of it so I can at least sleep at night."

To my horror, Dinah set the receiver down on the counter, emptied the vial into the palm of her hand, and tossed the pills into her mouth.

I reached for her and cried, "Dinah, no!" But she she'd already begun to chew the capsules and was managing, albeit with some difficulty, to swallow them.

I watched, frozen, as Dinah picked up the receiver again. "You took my husband and my son, Mr. Hunter. You may as well have me, too." Within seconds, she began to totter in the chair. The receiver dropped from her hand and hung by its cord to sway back and forth in mid-air. The alcohol and whatever else she'd consumed that morning, along with the fact that she'd broken the capsules with her teeth, served to speed up and intensify the effects of the pills; her eyes were already beginning to roll back into her head.

A jolt of electricity coursed through my brain, bringing me to my senses and spurring my body to action. I raced to the door, where Lyle the guard was stationed outside. I could see the top of his balding head through the small glass window, but he was facing the other direction, and the door wouldn't budge. I pounded it with both fists and screamed, "Help me, please!"

Lyle finally turned to face the door, his face at first reflecting confusion, then shock. I heard the buzzing and the click of the door as he opened it and rushed into the room. Two other guards I hadn't seen before followed close on his heels.

I shouted at them. "Do something! Call 9-1-1!"

A familiar voice yelled, "What, in God's name, happened here?!" Detective Staatz appeared in the doorway and, with disbelief, surveyed the scene before him.

I ran to him, grabbed his arm, and pulled him into the room. "Dinah swallowed some pills…a lot of pills. It happened so fast, I couldn't stop her."

The guards had Dinah stretched out on the floor. Staatz knelt down and felt her throat. "Her pulse is thready." He looked first to one guard, then to the other. "Do we know what she took?" His voice was strained with agitation.

The guard held up the empty vial. "This says Xanax, .5 mg."

"She'd already been drinking when she picked me up this morning," I said numbly.

"And you still let her go through with this? You let her drive?" Staatz's reprimand cut me to the bone. "Do you know how many she took?"

I shook my head. "The bottle looked to be at least half-full."

Paramedics hustled into the room with cases of emergency equipment and a gurney, and Staatz said, "Come on, let's give them some room."

I'd almost forgotten about Anthony Hunter. Just before leaving the visiting area, I turned to look at him. He hadn't moved from his seat at the table. The muscles in his face drawn taut, he observed the bizarre scene in front of him as though it were a horror film unfolding on a movie screen. He still held the phone receiver in his right hand.

In the front reception area, Staatz and I watched as paramedics hurried Dinah out the door and lifted her gurney into the back of an ambulance. We stood outside the entryway as it took off with lights flashing and sirens blaring, not budging until we could no longer see it or hear it.

"Can you take me to the hospital?" I asked. "I have to be with her."

"Why didn't you just take her keys and drive the Audi to the hospital?"

"I—I don't drive."

His face reflecting annoyance, he studied me for a long moment. I knew exactly what he was thinking: *What normal adult in this day and age doesn't drive?*

"Let's go, then. I'll have someone pick up the Audi and drive it back to her house." Staatz opened the passenger door for me and said, "I pray to God that this Reynolds has more luck on her side than the last two Reynolds did."

Chapter Twelve

On the way to St. Joseph's Hospital, Staatz remained silent and concentrated on wending his way through the sea of cars and semis that were all fighting for their places on the freeway during the beginning of the rush hour. I focused on the beauty of the desert, with its endless array of cacti and mountains softened by clouds of mist, on either side of us. I spotted a roadrunner as it dashed from one shrub to another; except for the frantic movement amid the abject stillness of its habitat, the bird's mottled brown form would have been invisible to me against the neutral hues of the sandy ground. This was life as it was intended: nature's splendor in all its glory, wrapping us in warm cloaks of serenity as we passed through. The murder of an innocent boy and the attempted suicide of a best friend had no place here. "I hate this," I said, absently watching a trio of hawks circle above the road.

"Excuse me?"

"Sorry. I didn't mean to say that out loud."

"You hate the traffic, Mrs. Winters?"

I shook my head. "No...well, yes. I do hate the traffic, but even more, I hate this ugly turn my life has taken."

Staatz gave me a wry glance. "*Your* life? It seems to me that it's Dinah Reynolds' life that's taken a turn for the worse."

Embarrassed, I hung my head. "You're absolutely right. I have this horrible habit of seeing everything through Amanda-colored glasses."

"Have you always had your, uh…" he grasped for the appropriate words.

"It's called Cluster C: a personality disorder, mind you—not a mental illness." I smiled weakly. "That should make me feel better, but it doesn't. To answer your question, the anxiety started when I was a child, although I didn't have my first full-blown panic attack until I was 16. Back then, I didn't know what it was…I don't think anyone did."

"Sixteen…that's a tough age, under the best of circumstances. It must have been rough."

"It was. I was walking to school when I suddenly became this tiny dot surrounded by strange houses, people I didn't recognize… Everything—even the air around me—became a part of some weird, alien landscape. The next thing I knew, I was in the eye of some horrible, private tornado, watching things spin around me…positive that at any moment my heart was going to burst through my chest."

"Wow, that *is* rough."

"I remember, if you'll pardon my crudeness, puking my guts out and hugging the pavement. Somehow, gravity had been reversed. I was actually afraid that I would fall off the Earth and go hurtling into space."

"Then what did you do?"

"As soon as everything stopped spinning, I got up from the sidewalk, dusted myself off, and went to school."

"Do you know the cause? Is it genetic?"

"Some experts believe that it might be. One psychologist chalked it up to the fact that I never bonded with my mother." I explained, "I spent the first ten months of my life in a state children's home. I was adopted."

He pulled onto an exit ramp and was forced to stop at a red light but nevertheless continued with the questioning. I was starting to feel uncomfortable…it never had been easy for me to talk about my Cluster C with people who were close to me, let alone someone I'd known for only a week.

"Were you ever agoraphobic?" he asked.

I narrowed my eyes and said, "Yes, that's a part of it. You're familiar with it?"

The light turned green, and he kept his gaze firmly fixed on the road ahead. "My mother had it. After my father died, she refused to leave the house. She didn't drive, didn't go out with friends, gave up church…gave up everyone and everything, really."

"That's awful. Is she still alive?"

He nodded. "She's in a nursing home."

"There was a time when I couldn't make it past my door as far as the mailbox. Now, the agoraphobia is just a general discomfort whenever I'm out and about. I'm okay as long as I have someone with me…someone I trust."

He looked at me with concern. "Do you trust me?"

"Yes, actually, I do." I paused for a moment to consider whether I should ask my next question, and decided that turnabout was fair play: It was time for the detective to do a little soul-spilling of his own. "Detective Staatz, have you ever been married?"

He fidgeted a bit in his seat, and then said, "Twice married, twice divorced." He laughed dryly and shook his head. "I guess I'm something of a stereotype. In all the movies, cops are divorced, bitter alcoholics." He added quickly, "Except I'm not all that bitter…or an alcoholic."

"I'm glad to hear that," I said, nodding. "Do you have any kids?"

He shook his head. "I never got that lucky, I'm afraid."

We pulled in front of the entrance to the ER, and Staatz reached over to push the door open for me.

"Aren't you coming in?" I asked.

"I'll be stopping by later. Right now I have a date with your aunt. After that, I'm meeting with Steven Bryce and Dieter Imfeldt."

"Well, good luck with Aunt Sally," I said. "You're in for quite an experience." Before I pushed the door closed, I leaned in and said, "Detective Staatz, why did you warn me to stay away from Aaron Hunter?"

"No specific reason."

I didn't believe that for a minute. "Anthony Hunter claims he's innocent. He said he didn't kill Nathan. He also said that he and Tom became friends before Tom disappeared...that Tom had found evidence that would incriminate Imfeldt, evidence that he planned to introduce at the tribal hearings."

"Yeah? Well, it's too bad Reynolds isn't around to corroborate that story." With that, he tossed me a half-wave and drove off.

*****

Inside the darkened ICU, blue lights glowed eerily, illuminating hospital personnel who spoke in hushed voices and moved intently from alcove to alcove, patient to patient. In one of the tiny curtained niches, in a narrow bed, lay Dinah. She was covered with a thin white blanket, and her head was propped up on two small pillows. Her lips were chalky, her normally beautiful olive complexion a grayish green.

A nurse wearing a coral smock and lipstick to match was adjusting an IV drip at the bedside. She spotted me and drew the curtain closed behind her. "Are you a family member?"

"Uh...yes. How is she?"

"We'll have to wait and see. Dr. Randolph's about to perform a gastric lavage."

I flashed her a questioning look.

"He's going to pump her stomach."

A physician who looked barely older than Jeff—Dr. Randolph, I presumed—asked the nurse if everything was ready as he swept past us. The nurse gave me an encouraging smile. "Why don't you go get a cup of coffee? There's a vending machine in the waiting area. It's pretty good…you can even get cappuccino."

"Thanks. Maybe I'll give it a try." I followed the signs to the waiting room and paused at the entrance to get my bearings before stepping inside. Thankfully, there were only two other people in there; if the room had been crowded, I would have turned around and looked for somewhere else to wait, preferably a secluded corner at the end of the hallway. I centered myself by focusing on the speckled black floor tiles, got my cup of coffee, and settled in a chair opposite the door. I was just becoming engrossed in an article about Scottsdale's ten most luxurious homes when the pages were abruptly cast into the shadow of someone who now stood in front of my chair.

"Terry!" I dropped the magazine and buried myself in his arms. After he pried me loose several minutes later, he asked how Dinah was.

"I don't know yet. They're pumping her stomach."

The Reades showed up next. They hurried into the waiting area, Carolyn looking as though she hadn't had a decent night's sleep in days. Frank didn't look much better.

I related the events leading up to Dinah's overdose. "I'm so sorry…I never saw it coming," I said. "I should have."

Dr. Randolph entered the room just then and walked toward us. "She's going to be all right," he said.

Frank Reade sighed heavily and Carolyn, relieved, rested her head on his shoulder.

The doctor added, "We're going to keep her overnight for observation. I suggested to her, however, that she seek counseling for depression, and for the substance abuse." He studied all our faces and added, "She'll need a lot of support."

"She'll have it," said Frank. "Whatever she needs, she'll have it."

We waited an hour or so as Dinah was moved to a bed on a regular medical floor. Dr. Randolph said that we'd be able to go into the room two at a time, but only for a few minutes. The Reades were taking the first turn when Detective Staatz joined us in the waiting area.

"How did your meeting with Aunt Sally go?" I asked.

"Not the best...I managed to get a description of the back of the intruder's head. And I had an interesting meeting with Bryce—I'll be taking a closer look at him—but I never got to talk to Dieter Imfeldt."

"Why not?" I asked, somehow knowing what the answer would be.

"Because he's dead...a gunshot wound to the head. A maid found him in his library this morning. It looks like suicide."

Chapter Thirteen

We'd spent less than ten minutes with Dinah at the
hospital. I wouldn't call it a visit; all Terry and I did
was to stand at the bedside and watch her sleep until
Pastor Mike arrived, looking a bit disheartened but
nevertheless determined. As we started for the door, he
opened his Bible to the Book of Psalms and began to
read. I hoped that the comforting words would reach
into Dinah's consciousness and soften her heart enough
to deal resolutely with all the pain that had been tearing
at her mind.

On our way to the elevator, the Reades intercepted
us in the hallway to tell us they'd like to stop by the
boys' apartment the next day and collect Nathan's
things.

"Of course," I said, thinking that for these
grandparents, the apartment visit would be the closing
act in this particular tragedy. Tomorrow in Nathan's
room, Carolyn Reade would still be able to hold a shirt
or a sweater to her face and inhale the scent of her
grandson; Frank Reade would be able to leaf through
the pages of a textbook left behind on a desk and, in
anguish, wonder why Nathan chose to highlight one
line over another. After tomorrow, the Reades'
connection with their only grandson would be reduced
to fading memories, occasional visits to the cemetery,
and sad glimpses of objects from the fleeting past:
grade school drawings and class photographs.

Early that evening, I settled on the patio with a glass
of wine and watched the deepening sunset turn our
neighbor's white house into a pink fairytale cottage that

sparkled like freshly spun cotton candy. The temperature was unseasonably warm, and I'd insisted that we take advantage of it by dining alfresco. With Jeff assisting as sous chef, Terry was breaking in the new gas grill with salmon fillets and thick slices of sweet potato drizzled with olive oil.

Conversation during dinner was sparse. What little of it there was centered on how great the new grill worked and the health benefits of salmon, largely a response to the fact that the results of my blood tests had come back to show that my cholesterol levels were a wee bit out of whack.

"This will give your HDL a boost," said Terry.

"Is that a good thing?" I asked. "I keep forgetting which is the good kind and which is the bad kind."

"HDL is the good kind. Just think 'H' for healthy and, in the case of LDL, 'L' for lousy."

Jeff told us that he was going to meet the Reades at the apartment the next afternoon. "I'm moving back there tomorrow, anyway," he said. "It won't take long to pack up Nate's stuff. I mean, he didn't have much. He still kept most everything at his mom's house." I could see the muscles in his jaw tense as he asked, "Will Mrs. Reynolds be all right?"

"The doctor thinks so," I said.

We ate in silence for a long while.

Finally Terry said, "So, Jeff, have you given any thought to what you'll do about the apartment? I hate to bring this up now, but I know there's no way you'll be able to swing the rent on your own."

His face weary, Jeff shrunk back into his chair. "I put myself on the list for a single room at one of the dorms. There are a few available...I'm just waiting to hear which one I can move into."

I reached across the table and placed my hand on top of his. "We'll miss you, you know. It's been wonderful having you here."

"Thanks." He flashed a tired smile and took his empty plate inside to the kitchen.

"Can we talk about the elephant now?" I asked Terry.

"What elephant would that be?"

"The elephant that Staatz let loose in the hospital today: Dieter Imfeldt's so-called suicide."

Terry, wine glass in hand, rested his elbows on the table. "You know what I think? Imfeldt was a sick old man. He was also a rich old man. People like Imfeldt—their whole lives, they get everything they want. When that changed—when his health failed, and he couldn't buy himself out of it—he couldn't accept it."

"You're saying Imfeldt couldn't accept the fact that he was dying, so he decided to hurry things up a bit by shooting himself in the head?"

Terry shrugged and refilled our wine glasses. "Exactly."

"Staatz said that Imfeldt's death 'looked like suicide.' What do you suppose he meant by that?"

"Only that he can't say it was suicide until the medical examiner officially rules that it was." His smile was grim. "They'll be doing an autopsy, sweetheart, so you don't have to worry that something will be missed. If Imfeldt was murdered, we'll know soon enough."

"Nathan may have met with Imfeldt, and now, less than two weeks later, both of them are dead. I think it's more than possible that their deaths are connected."

"Murder isn't contagious, Amanda," said Terry. "Even if you buy the idea that Aaron Hunter is carrying out some ten-year-old feud over his mother's death...that he killed Tom, then Nathan, and now

Imfeldt…why would he bother to make Imfeldt's murder look like suicide?"

"For the obvious reason—to divert attention from himself. Even if Anthony Hunter's poker game is nothing more than a lie cooked up by a few close friends, the fact is he probably won't be charged. He has an alibi; his son, on the other hand, doesn't. Aaron has to know that Staatz will be taking a close look at him once his father is cleared."

"There was an article about Imfeldt in yesterday's *Republic,*" said Terry. "His car collection alone is worth millions. Word is, Jay Leno's already put a bid in on the whole lot." He leaned back comfortably in his chair. "For the sake of argument, let's say that Imfeldt *was* murdered. You'd have to consider the possibility that plain, old-fashioned greed was the motive, and that someone in the family decided to free up their inheritance sooner rather than later."

"I suppose that's possible," I conceded. "But like you said, Imfeldt was sick. If someone stood to gain financially from his death, why not just wait for him to die?"

"Some relatives have no patience." Terry cradled the back of his head with his hands. "Okay, let's narrow things down: Anthony Hunter is locked up. He couldn't have murdered Imfeldt. So now the spotlight's on Aaron Hunter. Even if he is the murderer—I'm talking Nathan's murder, now—why would he frame his own father by stashing Nathan's bike behind his house?"

"I haven't figured that out yet."

"Amanda, I love you very much, so I want to make this clear: It's not your job to figure it out. Let it go. Let Staatz do his job, and just stay out of it. No one should ever want to get this close to murder."

"The truth is, murder got close to me, Terry…to us. Today I watched my best friend try to kill herself, and I was helpless to stop her. I don't want to be helpless anymore." I set my glass down and folded my hands purposefully on the table in front of me. "Will you take me back to the jail to see Anthony Hunter?" I was painfully aware of the irony of making that particular request on the heels of my "helpless" speech: I should be able to simply get into a car and drive to the jail if and when I chose to do so.

He shook his head. "Not a chance. I never should have let you go the first time."

"*Let* me go?! Did I hear you right?!"

Bolting upright in his chair, Terry turned into a defensive boy who'd just been caught with his hand in the cookie jar. "You know I didn't mean that the way it sounded."

"My mind's already made up. One way or another, I'm going to go back to that jail. Terry, Staatz has the wrong Hunter locked up. I'm sure of it."

While Terry was busy cleaning the grill, I snuck into the house to call Aunt Sally. "If you drive me on an errand Monday morning, I'll treat you to lunch."

"Lunch? Where?"

"Your choice."

"I wouldn't mind trying that new place in Tempe—Giovanni's. I heard they have a terrific accordion player." Her voice turned melancholy. "But he probably won't be playing during the lunch hour. Accordion music always sounds better in the dark."

"Giovanni's it is...accordion or no accordion."

"You got a deal!"

I sat down at my computer and pulled up the criminal records website for Arizona. After nearly half an hour, I still couldn't find anything related to Aaron Hunter. What had Staatz meant when he'd told me he had reasons for warning me to stay away from the younger Hunter? If Hunter had never been charged with a felony or misdemeanor, then what *had* he done to make Staatz think he might be a threat?

I called Dinah's landline number, and Carolyn Reade answered. They would be picking Dinah up from St. Joseph's the next morning. "I'm going to stay with her while Frank goes to the apartment for Nathan's things. Jeff's going to meet him there at noon."

I told her I'd call sometime tomorrow to check in on Dinah and went into the kitchen to help clean up. Jeff, however, had beaten me to it. I was thrilled to learn that, after loading the dishwasher, he and Terry had unpacked a few more boxes.

"Thanks, guys," I said. "I might just have to hire you both on a permanent basis. Anyone up for a cup of tea?"

"No thanks. I'm going to crash." Jeff reached out and gave me a good-night hug. "Love you, Mom."

"Love you, too. See you in the morning."

Terry and I took our tea to the living room and settled in front of the TV.

"I'm sorry about that whole 'letting you go' thing," he said. "But honestly, Amanda…murder is nothing to fool around with. It's better left to the professionals. They have guns."

"Anthony Hunter is safely behind bars. So what harm can just talking to him do?"

"Maybe you should ask Dinah that question."

*****

The weekend came and went without fanfare. Terry and I spent most of it rearranging furniture, hanging pictures, and looking at paint swatches. We'd decided to redecorate the house one room at a time, beginning with the kitchen. That Sunday afternoon, after changing my mind five times about what color the kitchen walls should be, Terry threw his arms up, said, "How about we just relax for the rest of the day?" and, despite his heartbreak over the fact that the Cardinals hadn't made it to the playoffs, turned on football. I picked up a crossword puzzle to keep my mind occupied during the game, the rules of which Terry had patiently attempted to explain to me numerous times without success. Instead of using the clues to fill in the little squares, however, I penciled in words related to Nathan's murder and to his father's disappearance: bicycle, cotton, DDT, April 18, Nathan's meeting with ?, emailed threats, Hunter Sr., Hunter Jr., Steven Bryce, Dieter Imfeldt, suicide…

*****

Terry and Jeff had left for work and school, respectively, by the time Aunt Sally and Arnold appeared in our driveway Monday morning. Once again, I felt the sting of my driving phobia and the loss of independence that came with it. A 72-year-old woman could, without a second thought, breeze her way through the 101 and 202 Phoenix loops in a Cadillac convertible, but I couldn't even bring myself to drive two blocks to the supermarket. I slid into the front passenger seat and waited for Aunt Sally to back out of the drive.

"Where to?" she asked.

"The Tempe jail on East 5th."

"You're kidding, right?"

"Nope. I need to talk to Anthony Hunter, the man they arrested for Nathan's murder."

"I thought you already did that."

"Actually, Dinah did that. But now I have a few questions of my own."

Aunt Sally clearly had an aversion to bars…at least the kind that criminals were placed behind. Claiming she wanted to do some browsing at the Tempe Library down the block, she dropped me off in front of the jail. "I'll pick you up right here in half an hour." She gave an exaggerated shiver. "I hate jails almost as much as hospitals and nursing homes. You're not going to do anything half-baked, are you? Like shoot Hunter for making Dinah try to kill herself?"

"Of course not."

Inside, I went through the same routine that Dinah and I'd been subjected to during our last visit. Lyle, the doorkeeper who'd come to my rescue three days before, unlocked the door for me. "How's your friend?"

"She'll be okay," I said, silently adding *at least physically*. "Thanks for asking."

Anthony Hunter sat in the same chair he'd used during the last visit. His right hand was on the telephone in front of him.

I picked up the receiver. "You haven't been sitting there all weekend, have you?" My joke was a feeble attempt to lighten the atmosphere, more so for me than for him.

"Is Mrs. Reynolds going to be okay?"

"Eventually."

"She didn't believe me when I told her that I didn't kill her son, or her husband."

"No, she didn't. But I do."

He exhaled loudly into the phone and allowed his body to relax. "Thank you."

As I stared through the window at Hunter, I observed my reflection in the glass and noted the discomfort that was clearly apparent on my face. I tried to think of the best way to discreetly ask my first question. Finally, I gave up and stormed ahead. "Mr. Hunter, do you think it's possible that your son murdered Nathan Reynolds?"

He shook his head vehemently. "No... no!"

"But how do you think Nathan's bicycle wound up in the woods behind your house? If you didn't put it there, and Aaron didn't put it there...then who did?"

"Whoever killed the boy."

I sat back in the chair and took a deep breath. "...to frame you for his murder."

"Of course."

"So someone you know—or at least someone who knows you, who knows you'd be a likely suspect because of those emails you sent Tom—killed Nathan. If not your son, then who?"

"The same person who killed his father, I expect."

"You think Tom was murdered?"

"I know he was murdered. A few days before he disappeared, he told me he was planning on taking his wife and son to Disneyland when the hearings were over. He pulled the tickets out of his pocket and showed them to me—he was going to surprise them. Does that sound like a man who's planning to desert his family?"

"No, it doesn't..."

"Like I told you, Tom said he'd gotten evidence against his client...evidence that would prove Imfeldt had been bringing in shipments of DDT and using it on his cotton fields long after it had been banned in this country." His gaze penetrated mine head-on. "He promised me he would bring that evidence to the hearing that following week. I know he had every intention of keeping that promise. Tom Reynolds was a man of honor."

I leaned forward in my chair. "Do you know what kind of evidence he had?"

"He wouldn't say, but I got the idea he was talking about photographs...maybe a videotape."

Photographs or a videotape that might still be hidden somewhere in Dinah's house.

Lyle opened the door. "Five minutes, ma'am."

"I have one more thing that I can't quite wrap my brain around. Detective Staatz warned me to stay away from your son, and I can't understand why. Aaron was pleasant enough when I met him after Nathan's funeral, and from what I've been able to gather, he has no criminal record…at least not in this state."

Hunter's body stiffened again. He studied his hands and said, "You'll have to ask Aaron about that."

I stood up then, pulling the phone with me so that it hung suspended above the counter. "Look, Mr. Hunter. I lost my godson to murder last week, and I nearly lost my best friend to suicide the other day right here in this room. I'm trying to help you, but I can't do that without knowing the truth. Please tell me what Aaron did."

Hunter wiped perspiration from his brow with his left hand and, resigned, looked me squarely in the eye. "He was a minor, so the record was sealed. Ten years ago, Aaron tried to kill Dieter Imfeldt."

Chapter Fourteen

I left the jail in a daze. Anthony Hunter had no idea that the cotton magnate had been murdered in his own home the day before. If he had, never would he have revealed the fact that Aaron had tried to kill Imfeldt ten years earlier. I was now convinced that Anthony suspected—or perhaps knew—that his son murdered Nathan and that he was lying to protect him.

If Aaron, at age 16, had attempted to kill Dieter Imfeldt, he could also have attempted to kill Tom Reynolds…and been successful in that attempt. It seemed to me that the younger Hunter could be in the process of waging a full-fledged vendetta. Who remained on his list, I wondered, that was still alive? Did Dieter Imfeldt have any children or grandchildren? Had he left behind a widow? And then the obvious occurred to me: Dinah was the sole remaining member of Tom Reynolds' immediate family. She would be somewhere on Aaron's list. I'd have to contact Detective Staatz as soon as possible and somehow get him to at least consider the possibility. I'd also have to persuade him to arrange some police security for Dinah.

I spied Arnold in a parking spot that was shaded under the canopy of a tall Palo Verde tree, whose branches, within a month or two, would be bursting with lemon-yellow blossoms. As I made my way across the macadam lot, the skin on my hands and face began to crawl, and the air around me transformed from an invisible something to be breathed into a tangible something to be seen, a kaleidoscope of flickering colors and morphing shapes. Beneath my feet, the surface of the parking lot became an undulating sea of black ooze. I walked past a palm tree whose fronds, seconds earlier, had been softly fluttering in the breeze like baseball cards in the spokes of a bicycle wheel, but which now began to pitch wildly. This was the onset of a panic attack, and judging by its intensity, the mother of all panic attacks. I managed to reach Arnold and pulled open the passenger door.

"I'm having one of my attacks, Aunt Sally," I said as I literally crawled onto the front seat.

Aunt Sally, her eyes wide behind her glasses, asked, "What happened in there?"

"Nothing much," I lied. "These attacks come out of the blue, for no reason. This one will pass in a few minutes." I leaned over so that my head was clear of the car.

"Are you going to hurl?"

"I don't think so," I said, and immediately did just that.

All we could do was sit in the car and wait for the attack to run its course. Aunt Sally pointed out a family of Gambel's quail, their distinctive top knots bobbing as they marched along the top of the stucco wall that encircled the parking lot. I focused on the birds' progress, and when the last of them disappeared, I fixed my gaze on Arnold's dashboard and gripped the door handle to keep the car's interior from spinning around me.

Only 15 minutes had passed, but it seemed like an hour before my panic attack had subsided to the point where I felt up to being inside a vehicle moving faster than the pace of a dying snail.

"Do you still want to go to Giovanni's?" asked Aunt Sally.

"Of course," I said, pulling out a notepad and a pen. "A deal's a deal."

"Are you making a grocery list? Do we need to go to Fry's after lunch? Because I could use a few things."

"I'm making notes. I've been thinking about Nathan's murder, his father's disappearance, the Hunters...all of it. My thoughts are kind of muddled right now...maybe they'll make more sense if I see them on paper."

"Huh," quipped Aunt Sally. "This one thinks she's Jessica Fletcher." She started up the Caddy and said, "I'll tell you one thing. Jessica Fletcher never had an attack of the heebie-jeebies so bad she had to vomit in the street."

*****

I walked into the kitchen to find Jeff ironing. "I thought you'd moved back to the apartment."

"I did. But I don't have an iron." He cocked his head at me. "You don't look so good."

"Can you believe it? I completely forgot to put on makeup this morning."

I opened the fridge in hopes of finding something appealing to make for dinner. I'd managed to keep down a cup of minestrone at Giovanni's, but now that I was feeling better, I was craving pasta. I grabbed a ginger ale and took it to the kitchen table.

"Want one?"

"No thanks. I've got a Dew going here."

"If you're ironing a shirt, you must have something important coming up."

"I have a job interview tomorrow at Salty's Tropical Fish and More."

"Sounds promising."

"Yeah, well, I figure it's something to do—you know, for money."

I persuaded Jeff to stay for dinner, and he kept me company in the kitchen while I threw together a quick fettuccine Alfredo and a salad. When Terry came home and saw the dining room table set for dinner, he kissed me and said, "You found the candles!"

"They were in the box marked 'miscellaneous.' I now also know where my Culture Club cassettes and the refrigerator magnets are."

He took a step back and studied my face. "You look pale. Feeling all right?"

"Mom says she forgot her makeup today," said Jeff, "but I think she looks pretty good—just sick."

"Thanks for the compliment," I said, my gaze pinning him with a mock glare. "I think."

Terry studied my face, started to say something, then thought better of it. At the dinner table, I knew his jovial mood would burst like a water balloon once I fessed up to having Aunt Sally drive me to see Anthony Hunter. Nevertheless, I spilled everything, including Hunter's adamant denial that his son was involved in Nathan's murder. I also mentioned Aaron's attempt on Imfeldt's life ten years earlier and ended with a brief recount of my panic attack, using it as a segue into a description of my lunch with Aunt Sally at Giovanni's. I could see that Terry was champing at the bit to reprimand me for using poor judgment in going to see Hunter, but thankfully, he decided not to make an issue of it in front of Jeff.

"It was something I had to do," I said, twirling fettuccine around my fork. "And I'm glad I did. By the way, I have a call in to Detective Staatz."

Terry and Jeff both stared inquisitively at me.

"To let him know that he arrested the wrong person."

Jeff's fork stopped midway between his plate and his mouth. "So who *should* he have arrested?"

"Aaron Hunter."

"The kid?"

Terry cleared his throat. "He's hardly a kid...he's almost thirty."

"Twenty-six," I said.

"I don't get it," said Jeff. "Why him? I mean, I can see why he'd have a thing against Imfeldt, but why Nate?"

"I have my reasons," I said, having learned a thing or two from Staatz.

Jeff stood abruptly and picked up his plate. "I'm really not hungry, Mom. I need to get going, anyway."

"Do you want to take that with you? I know where the Tupperware is now."

"Sure. Thanks."

After we'd seen Jeff out the door, I said to Terry, "I upset him with all that talk about the Hunters, didn't I?"

"Well, it doesn't take much these days."

"Will he be all right? Maybe he should have stayed here another night."

"He'll be fine."

More famous last words.

*****

Detective Staatz returned my call just as Terry and I were about to take a second glass of wine out to the patio. After the first glass, I'd convinced myself that Staatz would have to accept my supposition. I mean, it was perfectly logical to *me*.

I cleared my throat and plowed right in. "Detective Staatz, I think you have the wrong man locked up. The wrong Hunter, I mean."

I heard a loud sigh at the other end of the phone, then the gurgling sound of liquid pouring into a glass. "Go on, Mrs. Winters," which I interpreted to be *Just hurry up and get this over with so I can finish my drink and watch some TV.*

"Did you know that Aaron Hunter tried to kill Dieter Imfeldt ten years ago? He was a minor, so all records related to the crime were sealed."

"Now, I know you didn't come across that information on the Internet."

"Aaron's father told me about it this morning."

"You went back to the jail?" I heard *drib, drib, drib* as more liquid was poured into the glass.

"You can't believe that it was a coincidence Dieter Imfeldt died last week from a gunshot wound to the head. It seems clear to me that Aaron decided to finish the job he started a decade ago and arranged the crime scene to make it look like a suicide."

"You watch too many old detective shows, Mrs. Winters. I'll bet you're even a *Columbo* fan."

"Well, yes, I am, as a matter of fact. But that's beside the point."

"The Imfeldt murder belongs to the Scottsdale PD. But don't worry…they'll let me know if Aaron Hunter turns up as a suspect in that case."

"Let me remind you that Anthony Hunter has an alibi. How many of his friends were in that poker game? Four—five? Seriously…would five old men tell the same lie and think they'd be able to keep their stories straight? Would five men well into the sunset of their lives risk being charged with obstruction of justice—or perjury?"

"We found Nathan Reynolds' bike stashed in the woods behind Anthony Hunter's house. We didn't find it behind his son's house."

"The bike had no fingerprints on it. Aaron could easily have removed his fingerprints before planting the bike on his father's property."

"Why would he do that? Why not stash the bike somewhere in Mesa or Casa Grande? Why not hide it somewhere in the mountains, or in the desert? Why frame his father?"

"I don't know yet. But believe me, he had a reason." *And I'm going to find it.*

"Frankly, it's beginning to look like a moot issue. There's no way that bike, which amounts to circumstantial evidence, is going to be enough to make a murder charge stick to either of the Hunters."

"Let's assume Anthony Hunter's alibi is valid. If Aaron Hunter was capable of murdering ten years ago, I'm thinking he may have tried to kill Tom Reynolds, too."

I thought I might have heard a tiny chuckle...or maybe whatever Staatz was drinking went down the wrong pipe. "Aaron Hunter was 16 when Tom Reynolds disappeared. Even if he did somehow manage to kill Reynolds without anyone knowing about it, a 16-year-old wouldn't have the sophistication to know how to get rid of the body...or the car. A '75 Triumph in mint condition would stick out like a sore thumb." He paused, and then added, "A beautiful, and very expensive, sore thumb."

"You forget that I have a son, Detective. Let me assure you, 16-year-old boys are a lot more sophisticated than you may think."

I could tell he was getting ready to cut me off and end the call. He brushed aside my theory by saying that he'd already talked to Aaron several times and that bringing him in for more questioning now could be considered harassment. I asked him if he'd had a chance to check out both the Hunters' phone records for calls to or from Nathan's phone. He didn't take kindly to that question.

"Of course I have...give me some credit here, Mrs. Winters."

"So we're back to square one?"

"You, Mrs. Winters, are not back to anywhere. Hold on a minute...I've got another call coming in."

A few minutes later, Staatz clicked back onto the line. "You and Mr. Winters better meet me down at the substation. Your son was just picked up for assault."

*****

Ten minutes later, Terry and I were on the I-10 and heading to Tempe.

"Why aren't you moving over to the HOV lane?" I asked, noting that we had 15 minutes of rush hour to spare.

"Because I'd have to pull in behind that Prius—trust me, we'll make better time in the regular lanes with all the speeders."

I craned my neck to see around the minibus ahead of us. "Why are we stopping?"

Terry picked up on the fact that my breathing had started to quicken. "There must be an accident up ahead. Sit back and try to relax," he said, reaching over and patting my hand.

Although the traffic eased up enough to allow us to travel at the posted speed, the sun had long set by the time we arrived at the Tempe station. Jeff was being questioned by Judith Harvey, one of the officers who'd responded to our call the day the boys' apartment had been ransacked. I was relieved to see that my son wasn't wearing an orange jumpsuit, handcuffs, or manacles. He did, however, have a black eye, and his upper lip was swollen and bloody. Aaron Hunter, seated in a chair next to a desk at the other end of the room, was talking to Officer McNeary, Harvey's partner, who was using the hunt-and-peck method to fill out a form on the screen in front of him.

I rushed to the front counter. "Jeff!" Both Jeff and Aaron reacted to my cry with startled looks. Despite the circumstances, I found it odd to see Jeff in the role of the criminal. It was even odder to see Aaron Hunter in the role of the victim, considering it was quite possible that he'd murdered two, maybe three, people.

"Wait here a moment." Detective Staatz left Terry and me to stand at the front desk while he circled around it and motioned Harvey and McNeary to join him. After Staatz poured himself a cup of coffee, the three moved in a tight cluster to a far corner of the room like worker ants carrying a breadcrumb to the nest.

Terry placed firm hands on both my shoulders as if he thought I was going to leap over the counter and rush to Jeff's side. We couldn't hear anything that was being said: I tried to read Officer Harvey's lips, but to no avail. She shook her head, nodded, then shook her head again. Her gestures and body language didn't give me the tiniest clue as to where this thing was headed.

"I hate to say it, but I'm glad that Jeff's the one who got the worst of it," whispered Terry. "Hunter doesn't seem to have a scratch on him."

"Do you think he'll press charges?" I whispered back.

"I don't know, but I think we're about to find out."

Just then, Terry's cell phone rang, playing "You've Got a Friend," Dinah's ring tune.

My body responded with a nervous jerk. "I can't take any more bad news right now."

He handed the phone to me. "You have no idea why she's calling, sweetheart. She needs you…talk to her."

I took the phone and slipped out the front door. "Dinah…" My voice was weak with dread, my head buzzing with premonitions of the newest horror I was surely about to hear.

"Amanda! I'm so glad I was able to reach you." There was a pause. "Are you okay?"

"I'm fine. I'm sorry I didn't call earlier."

"Not a problem…I just got back from dinner with my parents. They're headed back to Tucson. Can you come over? Like right now?"

"I'm not exactly at home. Terry and I are…running an errand."

"When will you be home?"

"Soon, with any luck. What's wrong?"

"Amanda, I'm sure that someone's been watching my house…and he's outside right now."

Chapter Fifteen

Detective Staatz advised us that Jeff might require stitches, which meant another trip to the hospital. I told him about my conversation with Dinah, and he walked over to the desk sergeant. "Eddie, find the closest squad to the Reynolds place and have them check things out to make sure Mrs. Reynolds is all right."

Aaron Hunter decided not to press charges, and I was pretty sure it was because he didn't want to make an issue of the speck in Jeff's eye, what with the plank in his own. Since Hunter had sustained no injuries, Detective Staatz decided to let Jeff off with a strong warning. "If you come within a hundred feet of Aaron Hunter again, you will be arrested, and I'll make darn sure you do jail time."

"Is Hunter taking out a restraining order?" I asked.

"No. Consider this a personal arrangement between me and Jeff."

Terry led our son out to the car to lick his wounds while I stayed behind to apologize to the man I suspected of murdering my godson. *Keep your enemies closer,* I reminded myself.

"Aaron, I'm sorry."

Aaron Hunter's dark gaze penetrated mine. "Keep your son away from me, Mrs. Winters. Next time, he'll need more than a few stitches."

"Consider it done." I started to turn toward the front entrance, then paused. "I believe your father's innocent, you know. I don't think he murdered Nathan."

Aaron shrugged. "It really doesn't matter to me what you think. Staatz knows that someone planted that bike behind my father's house. He'll be out of jail soon."

I folded my arms in front of me for an extra measure of stability and took a deep breath. "I think you're the one who planted the bike in your father's yard. I also believe you murdered Nathan and Tom Reynolds, and I intend to prove it."

"You're freakin' crazy!" Aaron took a step toward me. Every muscle in his face and neck pulsed, and he began to flex his hands nervously: fingers open, then closed, and open again.

"That temper that got you into trouble ten years ago—you still have it, don't you?"

"*I* have a temper?" he said with a dry laugh. "I've never jumped anyone in a supermarket parking lot."

"You know what? I don't know what's worse, the fact that you may have, and I use the term 'may have' loosely, killed three people in cold blood, or the fact that you'd frame your own father for the murders you committed."

Aaron glanced over at Detective Staatz, who had been watching us with growing concern. Staatz cocked his head and said, "Everything all right over there?"

"Everything's fine," I said calmly. But, given the skeptical look on his face, I hadn't fooled Staatz. I turned back to Aaron and said, "Dieter Imfeldt died last Friday...but I think you probably already knew that. They're saying it looks like suicide. Your first attempt to kill Imfeldt failed...but this time you got it right, didn't you? Aaron, if you decided to finish the job you started a decade ago, why don't you just come clean about it right now, for your father's sake?"

I could almost feel the heat of the blood pumping through his veins. Hunter was seething mad, and he wasn't doing a very good job of hiding the fact. At that moment, I realized just how lucky Jeff had been to escape with the few injuries he had.

Though I supposed it might be a good idea to hightail it out of there post-haste, I summoned my most dignified manner and tried to keep my steps slow and easy as I walked out the door. I wanted to stir the hornet's nest and force Aaron's hand, and by the looks of it, I'd been successful. Now I'd just have to wait for his next move. Hopefully, Staatz would be there to see it and take appropriate action...like putting the younger Hunter behind bars and releasing his father.

In the car, I had little to say to Jeff. I couldn't really fault him for what he'd done: His actions were the direct result of our conversation at the dinner table, a conversation I'd initiated. I'd accused Aaron Hunter of Nathan's murder, and, Jeff's anger simmering below the surface since tragically losing his best friend, had prompted him to take care of the matter himself. He obviously hadn't given any thought to the fact that Hunter's six-feet two-inch, 200-pound physique would prove a potentially deadly threat to his own five-feet ten-inch, 155-pound frame.

"Jeff, what were you thinking?" Terry said as we got into the car. "What if he'd been carrying a gun?"

"I'm sorry...I guess I wasn't—thinking."

"I'm glad you came to that conclusion," I said. "So did you just happen to run into Hunter at the grocery store?"

"I was driving past his house and saw his truck pull out."

"How do you even know where he lives?"

"He was visiting his dad at the jail this morning, and I followed him home. He lives just off Riggs Road, in a trailer on the edge of the reservation."

"What were you doing at the jail?"

"I dunno. I guess I just wanted to see if they'd let me talk to Anthony Hunter...the old guy." He peered out from the eyes of a forlorn child. "No one ever tells me anything. I couldn't even get up the nerve to go inside."

I turned around to kneel on the front seat and took his hands. "I'm sorry. What do you want to know?"

"Who killed my best friend, and why."

I squeezed his hands in frustration. "We don't have those answers yet."

"But we will," said Terry. His lips were tight as he admonished me with an intense gaze. "If we just keep out of his way, Detective Staatz is going to figure it all out." He started up the car. "In the meantime, you need to stay away from Aaron Hunter. Don't go near his house...and, as long as his father's locked up, don't go near the Tempe jail, either. A criminal police record for stalking isn't something you want to have to explain to potential employers. Hunter let you off easy today. I have no idea why he didn't press charges."

"Which brings me to my next question," I said. "Jeff, how are you going to explain that black eye at your interview tomorrow?"

He sank back into the seat and groaned. "I'll have to cancel it. I can't lie about it, and if I just ignore it, they'll think the worst anyway."

I asked Terry to drop me off at Dinah's house after he assured me that he'd be fine taking Jeff to the ER without me. "Detective Staatz sent a squad to check things out at Dinah's," I said. "By the way, I think Staatz may have more than a professional interest, there."

"Sweetheart, romance is the last thing on Dinah's mind right now."

"Of course, I know that. I'm just saying..."

As Terry walked me to Dinah's front door, the hairs on my arms stood on end. I used my peripheral vision to check out the immediate area, but I didn't see anyone. A few vacant cars, none of them resembling a police vehicle, were parked along the road, but there was nothing that looked to be out of the ordinary. I rang the bell, and Dinah answered immediately. To my relief, no tell-tale odor of alcohol oozed from her pores.

She offered a smile. "Thanks for sending the cavalry…they just left. Unfortunately, the guy took off before they arrived."

We watched as Terry got into the car and, before driving off, motioned for us to get inside the house. Grabbing my hand, Dinah pulled me into the living room and slammed the door shut before sliding the dead bolt into place. Despite the fact that the outdoor temperature was in the high sixties, she'd started a fire in the fireplace. If the room had been the size of my living room, the air would have been stifling, but the majority of the heat wafted up to the vaulted ceiling and circulated to encompass us with a cozy warmth.

"I have a lot to say to you," she said.

Oh, boy, I thought, expecting another scolding or worse. *Here it comes.*

"Can you ever forgive me for putting you through that scene at the jail?"

"You only need to forgive yourself. No apologies needed here."

Her deep brown eyes were clear and sad. "Regardless, I apologize. You don't deserve to be treated the way I've treated you these last few days. I've got an appointment to see someone…a psychologist. And Pastor Mike put me in touch with a grief support group in Chandler."

"That's the best news I've heard in a long time," silently adding *I hope you have better luck with psychologists than I ever did.*

"That moment at the jail, I wanted nothing more than to die. I still want to, in a way."

She saw the expression on my face and quickly added, "Oh, I'm not going to do anything stupid again. I'm just telling you how I feel. I want to be with Nate. I know that I can't, that I shouldn't...can you understand that?"

"Of course," I said, thinking of Terry and Jeff...and what I'd do if anything happened to either of them. I took her hand and squeezed it. "Now tell me why you think someone's watching the house."

She rose from the sofa and went to the window. "I've seen someone—a man—hanging around outside for a few days, now."

I joined her at the window and peered out into the darkness.

She drew the blinds and said, "Let's go into the kitchen. For some reason I feel safer there."

We sat at the island and drank Earl Grey from English bone-china cups embellished with tiny pink roses and rimmed with gold. I held a delicate saucer in my left hand and with my right held the cup to my nose to inhale its fragrant steam. "This man who's been hanging around...is he on foot or driving?"

"Driving a pickup...slowly...back and forth...then he stops in front of the house. Every night this week, now."

"And you don't recognize him?"

"He always comes when it's dark and parks in front of the streetlamp, so his face is in the shadows. He just sits there, sometimes for minutes, sometimes for half an hour. I never get a clear look at him, but I can tell that he's watching the house."

"Is it possible he's just a neighbor with insomnia?"

A faint smile played on her lips. "No, I'm sure that's not it. He studies the house as though—I don't know—on TV, they'd say he's 'casing the joint.'"

"What make of car?"

"Some kind of pickup truck...I can't tell one make from another. Black, I think."

Aaron Hunter drove a pickup truck, but his presence at the Tempe police station ruled out the possibility that he'd been the one lurking outside Dinah's house, at least on this particular occasion. Of course, it was still possible that he had an accomplice who took care of stalking duties when Aaron was busy with other things. But who? Staatz had said that the Pimas were a close-knit people: Aaron must have any number of friends who'd be willing to help him carry out his vendetta. Why did I have to be the only one to see the puzzle pieces falling into place, one by one? Why couldn't Staatz get into the act? At least he had the experience and the authority to be able to do something about it. Of course, Staatz might be seeing the same puzzle pieces falling into place and just keeping them to himself. I set my cup and saucer down and ran my hand along the cool surface of the island's granite top.

She walked over to the stove. "Want some more tea?"

"No, thanks. But you know what I'm going to say next, don't you?"

"You want me to call Detective Staatz and ask for some patrols outside my house. The thing of it is, after what I did at the jail, I'm too embarrassed. He probably thinks I'm a hopeless mental case."

I smiled. "I know for a fact that's not true."

The conversation turned to the Hunters. I came clean and told her everything: that I thought Anthony Hunter was covering up for his son, Aaron, and that I believed he killed Nathan as a part of some bizarre blood feud as payback for his mother's death.

"I went back to the jail and had another chat with Anthony Hunter," I said. "He told me that Aaron tried to murder Imfeldt ten years ago."

Dinah leaned forward with interest. "Are you serious?" She settled back again, and stared off into the distance. "If he was capable of attempting to murder Imfeldt, he'd also be capable of murdering Tom."

"My thoughts exactly. I brought the possibility up to Staatz. We'll just have to wait and see what he does with it. Since Aaron was only 16 at the time, the record's sealed. So the information probably can't be used in court anyway." I told her about Jeff's attack on Aaron Hunter in the parking lot and about my conversation with him at the police station. "Jeff did a stupid thing. He was lucky this time."

Dinah wrapped her hands around her cup as if to warm them. "He was luckier than Nate, that's for sure."

Feeling horrible about saying the wrong thing yet again, I turned the conversation back to my second visit with Anthony Hunter. "He said that Tom had found evidence against Dieter Imfeldt—evidence that would prove he was bringing in illegal shipments of DDT to use on his crops. 'Photos or a videotape,' he said."

I told her, then, about Tom's plans to take her and Nathan to Disneyland after the hearings. "The day before Tom disappeared, he showed Hunter the tickets."

Dinah's entire body seemed to collapse in on itself. "Then he wasn't planning to leave us."

"If you believe Hunter, it certainly doesn't look like it." I took our cups to the sink, rinsed them, then returned to lean against the island. "Dinah," I said with arms folded, "are you up to searching the house with me right now? I think that the evidence Tom found might still be here somewhere. I think Aaron Hunter trashed Nathan and Jeff's apartment because he was looking for it. If Hunter's having someone watch your house, he might just be waiting for the right time to pick up his search where he left off."

"Maybe we should call Detective Staatz before we go any further…"

I gave an impatient sigh. "Dinah, have you ever heard 'there's no time like the present'? I don't think we should wait for Staatz. I mean, he's sharp enough, but he isn't exactly a 'hell on wheels' kind of guy."

"I guess…"

"Anyway, I think that when Nathan found the notes, emails, and calendar page in that box, he set something in motion that had lain dormant for ten years. Aaron Hunter may initially have wanted to get his hands on that evidence so he could use it to incriminate Imfeldt…but then something Nathan did or said spooked him."

"Spooked him enough to kill him," said Dinah.

"Aaron must have been the one who broke into your garage. But when he couldn't find what he was looking for, he decided to take care of Imfeldt another way."

"By shooting him and arranging it to look like suicide. But why stash Nathan's bike in the woods behind his father's house?"

"I'm not sure, yet, but I think it's safe to assume that Aaron Hunter and Anthony Hunter are no longer hanging out on the same branch of the family tree."

Dinah's face was set with determination. "I couldn't care less whether Dieter Imfeldt was murdered, committed suicide, or was zapped into outer space by aliens. The only thing I care about right now is finding out who murdered my son and what really happened to Tom. If Aaron Hunter's behind all this, he needs to pay for what he's done."

"We have to find that evidence, Dinah. This whole thing started with Tom, and I think it's going to have to end with him."

Chapter Sixteen

I rubbed my hands together with exaggerated fervor. "Now…where should we start?"

Dinah shook her head slowly. "I don't know. I went through all Tom's things years ago, and I didn't come across anything out of the ordinary."

"You weren't expecting anything out of the ordinary ten years ago."

"Then I guess Tom's study is as good a place to start as any."

The study, which I suspected Dinah hadn't made the slightest change to since Tom's disappearance, was a richly appointed room with floor-to-ceiling bookcases and Brazilian cherry wood flooring. I studied the desk, a vintage mahogany library table that dominated the center of the room.

"Didn't Tom keep a computer in here?" I asked.

"We got rid of it years ago," Dinah said. "Nate and I both had our own computers, so we didn't see the need to hang onto it. Besides, we didn't have Tom's password, so we couldn't get into any of his documents even if we'd wanted to."

"What about the computer he used at work?"

"It was the firm's property, so they kept it."

"Tom probably didn't keep anything related to what he found against Imfeldt on either of those computers anyway," I said. "Anthony Hunter thinks Tom had photos or a videotape."

I studied the bookcases, and the excitement I'd felt only moments ago began to dissipate when I considered the sheer "volume of volumes" we'd have to wade through. "Photographs can easily be hidden inside books—we'll have to go through each one," I said.

"But there are hundreds!"

I stood up straight and stretched, hoping to muster enough energy cells, despite my fatigue, for the search. "Then we'd better get started. You take that end, I'll take this end, and we'll meet in the middle." I took one of the books from a shelf, opened it, and tipped it upside down so that its pages fanned open. "If we do it like this, it shouldn't take us more than an hour or two to get through the entire library."

Dinah moved toward the door.

"Where are you going?" I asked.

"We'll be working in here for a while. I'm making coffee…and I think there's a king-sized bag of M&Ms in the pantry with our names on it."

It felt good to see at least a tiny spark of Dinah's old sense of humor. I knew that grief would continue to shadow it for some time to come, but it was a hopeful beginning. I literally rolled up my sleeves and started the task at hand.

A pot of coffee and half a bag of M&Ms later, we'd finished searching the last shelf of books, but within those thousands of pages found nothing more than an old McDonald's cash receipt and an ad for an air-conditioning service that Tom had clipped from the *Phoenix Republic*. We made a cursory search of the rest of the library: the cabinets underneath the built-in bar, the credenza, and the drawers in two matching occasional tables.

"I told you," said Dinah, "there's absolutely nothing here."

"What about your bedroom closet?" I asked. "Did you save any of Tom's clothes?"

She shook her head. "I donated everything to Goodwill years ago." She saw the look on my face and added, "Don't worry. I went through all the pockets first."

After Dinah systematically eliminated all the other rooms in the house as potential hiding places, we moved on to the garage. I suggested we try Staatz's approach: Start in the middle and move slowly in increasing concentric circles to the outer perimeter.

Arms akimbo, Dinah studied the expanse of the three-car garage and asked, "Okay. How's this supposed to work?"

"We stand in the middle of the room with our backs to each other and let our eyes do the searching while we slowly pivot. Then we move a foot out and do it again. We repeat the process until we reach the exterior walls. We move everything on the shelves, look behind things, do whatever it takes to make sure we've covered every square inch of this garage." I put a hand on Dinah's shoulder. "You once told me that whenever Tom wasn't in his study, he was out here. Maybe we'll find something."

We'd just started our search when Dinah's cell phone went off. "It's for you...your Aunt Sally."

"Oh, Lord, now what?" It was already past ten p.m., and I knew that late-night phone calls generally meant that something catastrophic has happened. Things had gone horribly wrong at the ER: The physician administering Jeff's stitches had forgotten to sterilize the instruments, and Jeff had lapsed into some sort of infectious coma. Terry wouldn't want to break the news to me, and asked Aunt Sally to do his dirty work.

"Aunt Sally, what's happened?!" I asked. My heart was pounding, and my hands had already begun to perspire to the extent that Dinah's phone slipped from my grasp so that I had to catch it in midair.

"Terry told me you were at Dinah's. I have good news!"

I let out a deep sigh. "Can you give me the basics and fill in the details tomorrow? We're kind of in the middle of something here."

"I have a boyfriend. Ha! I'll bet you never expected to hear that!"

"A boyfriend…that's great. Do I know him?"

"Not yet…he just moved to Sun Lakes from Miami. His wife died a few years ago…lucky break for me."

"Aunt Sally, really!" I scolded. "Where did you meet this man?"

"After bridge club, Esther—you know Esther—she's my Jewish friend, her son's a podiatrist…"

"Details tomorrow, remember?" I rolled my eyes and shrugged an apology to Dinah.

"Anyway, after bridge, Esther and I went to the Cottonwood Club for cocktails, and he sat down on the stool next to me. His name is Ernest Saunders, but I call him Ernie, and we have a date for tomorrow night. He's taking me to karaoke."

"That's wonderful. Listen, I need to hang up now, but I promise to give you a call tomorrow, okay?"

"Make it the day after…I have a whole beauty regimen set up for tomorrow…mani/pedi, facial, body wave, the works. Besides, I might have some really good stuff to tell you after my date."

A day's reprieve, then. "I'll talk to you Wednesday."

Dinah and I continued what I'd come to think of as "the Staatz method." Using the detective's pivot technique, we reached the exterior wall after only 15 minutes. To search the wall cabinets and shelving, we used the same approach we'd used in the library. Dinah started with the wall on one side of the door, and I started with the other. I found a stepladder and dragged it along beside me so that I could use it to get a clear view of the shelving above eye-level.

"When you're finished with that ladder, I'll have another go-round at the higher shelves on my side," said Dinah.

"What's this?" I said, reaching for a small white box that I'd nearly missed. "Oh, never mind…it's just a box of picture hooks."

Dinah came over and stood next to the ladder. "That's strange."

"What, picture hooks?"

"Tom was obsessive about keeping the garage organized. He would never store picture hooks on a shelf with paint supplies. He would have put them on the shelf with the boxes of screws and nails."

The box was flat, but large enough to contain one videotape or a number of photographs. I picked it up and shook it. "You're right. These aren't picture hooks in here." I backed down the ladder carefully, the box firmly in my grip, and handed it to Dinah. "I'll let you do the honors."

"Let's take it into the house," she said, glancing over her shoulder at the garage door.

We entered the house through the back door into the kitchen. We didn't take time to sit; as soon as we were inside, Dinah locked the door behind us and lifted the lid from the box.

"Photos!" I exclaimed.

"Tom's evidence…hidden in plain sight," she said, lifting the pictures from the box. They were glossy black-and-whites, taken at night, so we had to squint closely to make out what we were actually looking at. Five men, their backs to the camera, seemed to be rolling large canisters off the ramp of a truck. In the background of one of the photos was what looked to be an entrance to a cave, where a number of the canisters had been placed.

"Those must be some kind of oil drums or something. And it looks like they're getting ready to move them into the cave," said Dinah. "Those are rails leading into it...I'll bet it's a mine—copper or gold—abandoned, by the looks of it."

Something was printed on the canisters, but even with the help of my readers, neither of us could make out the words. "Do you have a magnifying glass?" I asked.

"I gave it to Nate a few months ago for some class project he was doing." She closed her eyes, and I knew she was remembering that moment, reliving the conversation, every detail of it.

I asked her if I could take the pictures home and show them to Terry. "He might recognize something...he's seen a lot of news footage of the terrain around here."

"Only if I can come with you...I know these photos have been here for over a decade, but I don't want to wait another minute to find out what they have to do with Nate's death, if anything."

"I have to ask," I said tentatively. "You got rid of all Tom's clothes, but it never occurred to you, even once, to look through his things in the garage?"

"It's silly, isn't it? Clothes go out of style, but tools don't. I wanted to keep everything out there just as Tom left it...even the dust. Crazy, huh?"

I gave her a hug. "No...not crazy. 'Hopeful,' maybe."

We returned to the living room windows and examined the yard and driveway before letting ourselves out the front door. I was relieved to see that a timer had kicked in since my arrival: Several floodlights that Dinah had installed after the garage break-in illuminated the entire area as far as the road in front, their brilliance extending to merge with the neighbors' lighting on either side of the house.

"All clear," I said. Nevertheless, we were watchful as we hurried to the Audi, which Dinah had moved to the driveway prior to our search of the garage.

We were half-way to my house when she said, "Don't panic, but I think we're being followed."

I turned in my seat to look behind us. "Can you go faster? Let's see if they follow us when we make the turn up ahead."

Dinah pulled onto Alma School Road and headed south. It was now just before midnight, and there wasn't much traffic. I glanced in the side mirror: The vehicle had been following us at a steady pace, but it was now increasing its speed despite the fact that the stoplights ahead, at the intersection of Alma School and Riggs, had just turned red. White glare from the headlights flooded the Audi's interior just as we reached Riggs.

"Hold on," said Dinah. She gripped both sides of the steering wheel and veered sharply into the left-turn lane just in time to avoid a rear-end collision. The pickup screeched past us, zooming through the red light and barely missing a produce truck that was traveling east on Riggs. We watched as the taillights grew fainter in the darkness as the pickup continued to race toward the desert expanse of the Gila River Indian Reservation.

"Did you get a look at the driver?" asked Dinah, her voice coming in fits and starts as she tried to catch her breath.

"No," I said. "But that truck looks awfully familiar."

Chapter Seventeen

We found Terry stretched out on the sofa. He was covered with the afghan my mother had knitted 25 years ago from five different shades of blue yarn. The TV was on and tuned to one of the cooking channels: Rachael Ray was demonstrating the proper way to prep a baby octopus for an audience who would likely be too sleepy to be repulsed by the unappetizing process. I turned off the set, and Terry bolted upright in a confused state, not unlike a mummy who'd just awakened from the dead and was attempting to rise from its sarcophagus.

"Huh? Hey, I was watching that."

I bent down and kissed the top of his head. "It's me, sweetheart…I've got Dinah with me."

He rubbed the sleep from his eyes. "What time is it?"

"After midnight. We need you to take a look at something."

He freed himself from the tangle of afghan and said, "And I need to get to bed. I promised to spot Edwards for the morning show, which starts…" He wiped the sleep from his eyes and glanced at his watch, "…in less than five hours."

Dinah was still hovering awkwardly near the front door. I waved her into the room and said, "I suppose Tom's photos can wait till you get home tomorrow."

His ears pricked up like a Chihuahua responding to the cries of a hotdog vendor. "Tom's photos?"

Dinah sat down on the sofa next to Terry, lifted the lid from the little white box that held Tom's pictures, and handed the stack of photos to him. "We found these in the garage. Amanda thought you might be able to recognize the background terrain and help us determine where the photos were taken. We think that big hole in the side of the mountain is a mine entrance."

There were seven pictures in all, and Terry studied each closely for several minutes before saying, "You're right about that cave entrance being an adit. The mine looks to be pretty old, and from the state of those rails leading into it, it must have been abandoned long ago. But I have no idea where it might be located. I can't tell a thing from these pictures. They could have been taken anywhere in the Southwest."

"Can you at least make out what's written on any of those drums?" Dinah asked hopefully.

Terry held one of the photos up to his nose. "Nope."

"Hold on a sec." I went to the guest bedroom that did double-duty as my office and rummaged in the top desk drawer for my magnifying glass. Terry accepted it eagerly and squinted through the lens to examine the tiny print on the canisters. Dinah and I sat on either side of him, pressing in close to get a few good looks of our own through the glass.

"Those look like standard 55-gallon drums being unloaded from that truck. The number 1-9-9-7 is painted on this one. See?" He drew a few of the pictures closer to us and used the handle of the magnifying glass as a pointer. "I can make out the word 'VENENO' on these two, and there's 1-9-9-7 again, on that one."

"Veneno," I said. "What does that mean?"

"I used to help Nate with his high school Spanish," said Dinah numbly. "It means 'poison.'"

"Why do you think those two drums are numbered the same?" I asked.

"I'd say that the number is actually a production year: 1997."

"So whatever's inside those drums was manufactured in 1997?"

Terry shrugged. "Probably."

"Was DDT still being made then?" I asked.

"I'm not a hundred percent sure, but I think it was banned sometime in the eighties."

We went to the guest room that doubled as my office. Terry and Dinah sat on the edge of the bed, still unmade after Jeff's brief stay, while I Googled "DDT." We learned that the insecticide had indeed been banned in the United States and Canada in the 1980s, but that several countries continued to use it in areas where malaria was a major problem. It was first restricted, and then outlawed, in those countries after several studies indicated that the toxin builds up over time in the fatty tissue of animals and humans. It was also proved that, after settling in freshwater bodies and oceans, it becomes increasingly concentrated, thereby causing many different types of cancers and a host of neurological, respiratory, and cardiovascular illnesses in those who had the misfortune of eating tainted fish from the affected bodies of water.

"No wonder Tom hid the photos," said Dinah, her voice wavering. "He knew that Imfeldt would likely stop at nothing to keep them out of the hands of the tribal council."

"I'd guess that if it could be proved that Imfeldt was spraying his cotton crops with DDT after it was banned, he'd be open to quite a few lawsuits," I said.

"He'd also be open to federal prosecution for bringing an illegal substance across the border," added Terry. "Those drums had to have originated somewhere in Mexico."

I thought about Evelyn Hunter. I could easily understand how Anthony and Aaron might hold Imfeldt to blame for her death. For generations, the Hunter family had lived on the Gila River Indian Reservation. Established by an Act of Congress in 1859, the land, which borders Sun Lakes to the south and to the west, is home to, among other tribal factions, the *Keli Akimel O'otham*, or the "Gila River People," of the Pima community. Like his ancestors before him, Anthony Hunter had actively fished its streams and farmed its land, adapting the desert to his family's needs and, via the use of intricate irrigation systems, turning the arid landscape into a rich growing medium for crops such as corn, beans, and wheat. A map of the area clearly showed that Imfeldt's cotton fields were adjacent to the reservation's farmland, including the acreage worked by Hunter.

"Well, these photos certainly complicate matters," I said. "If Tom was going to bring these pictures to the tribal hearings, why would Aaron want him dead? Wouldn't he be happy about Tom introducing evidence that would prove Imfeldt's guilt?"

"Remember, Anthony Hunter was only guessing that Tom's evidence was photos," said Terry. "Back then, Aaron couldn't have known these pictures existed. At the time of the hearings, he was a troubled kid who'd just lost his mother."

"So as far as Aaron was concerned, Tom was still as guilty as Imfeldt," I said.

"And the only thing Nate was guilty of was being Tom's son," added Dinah sadly.

"There's still the possibility that both Hunters are innocent," I said. "Here's another thought. Imfeldt could have murdered Tom years ago, and, after getting that phone call from Nathan, thought he'd stumbled onto his father's evidence. It's likely that Imfeldt had no idea as to what that evidence was, exactly, but I'm sure he would have assumed the worse."

Dinah shook her head slowly. "Then he killed Nate to keep him quiet...and when he realized that Nate didn't have the photos after all, he realized what he'd done."

"And killed himself," said Terry, completing the scenario.

"Maybe," I said. "It's just one of many possibilities."

"Another possibility is that Anthony Hunter might be lying to protect his son," said Terry. He put the photos back inside the box. "Regardless, we should be handing these over to Staatz—like yesterday. Remember how upset he was over the emails..."

Dinah's face reddened. "I was upset, too. I'm sorry I blew up at you like that."

I gave her a reassuring smile. "Already forgiven and forgotten."

I switched off my computer, and we headed back into the living room. "If those drums are somewhere inside that mine and they really do contain DDT," Terry said, "the physical evidence might be enough to clear both Hunters. Imfeldt would be the prime suspect."

"Here's another problem I have with that," I said, deep in thought. "Imfeldt may have had motive, opportunity, and the strength to kill Tom a decade ago, but I don't think he'd have the agility to make it down that embankment to the river where Nate was shot." I glanced at Dinah. "Sorry."

"You two have to stop apologizing," she said, her voice straining to be audible. "We're never going to get to the bottom of this if you can't speak plainly in front of me."

"You're sure you're okay with all of this?" I asked. "If you want us to step back and let Staatz do all the digging around, all you have to do is give the word."

She shook her head slowly. "No. I appreciate that you're trying to find out what happened to Nate...and to Tom."

"Then we'll just hang onto these a little longer," said Terry. He offered to take the photos to work with him the next day to compare the background terrain with footage from the station's film archives. "I don't expect that I'll be able to pinpoint an exact location," he said, "but I might be able to come up with a general area." He cleared his throat and gave me a stern look. "And then we'll turn the pictures over to Staatz."

Dinah said, "Amanda, we haven't mentioned the truck."

"What truck?" asked Terry.

"The pickup truck that nearly ran us off the road," I said. "Someone followed us from Chandler to Sun Lakes. It must have been the guy Dinah noticed watching her house. He almost rear-ended us on Alma School—I'm not sure if he was trying to scare us or kill us—then ran a red light and headed south on Riggs toward the reservation."

Terry turned to Dinah. "Staatz doesn't have a patrol car stationed outside your place?"

"No," she said, her voice betraying a touch of resentment.

"Maybe it's time he did." Terry turned to me with a pointed look. "Aaron Hunter drives a pickup and lives on the reservation. Maybe he made a little side trip to Ocotillo Springs after leaving the Tempe substation."

"I'm calling Detective Staatz first thing in the morning," I said. "I'm sure he'll want to ask Hunter a few more questions."

"When you talk to him, don't mention the photos," said Terry. "Staatz would want us to hand them over right away—I think we'll hang onto them until we know where that mine is."

I gave his hand a little pat. "Withholding evidence, huh? It seems I'm having a bad influence on you."

Terry dismissed the remark with a wave as he stepped into his shoes. "Dinah, we're following you home."

*****

Tuesday

After a few hours of sleep and more hours of lying awake, I gave up, switched on the coffeepot, and decided to tackle the job of organizing the guest-room closet. I was standing on a stepladder and arranging stacks of linens on a shelf when the landline phone on my desk warbled loudly, nearly causing me to lose my balance. With some dread (*now what?!*), I climbed down the ladder, walked slowly to my desk, and picked up the phone. My breathing had already begun to come in quick, shallow bursts, and when I checked the screen and saw "Terry–WORK" flashing there, I collapsed onto the desk chair and forced myself to calm down for a few seconds. If Terry was calling me, it meant that he was at least well enough to make a phone call. I turned down the ringer volume and picked up.

"What's wrong?!" I asked.

There was a deep sigh. "Amanda, nothing's wrong. Everything's fine." But the disappointment in his voice was unmistakable. "I must have gone through at least five years' worth of video, and none of it offers the slightest clue about where Tom might have taken those photos."

"Oh," I said, feeling my heart sink. "Well, thanks for trying, anyway."

His voice picked up a notch as he added, "I didn't find the location of the mine, but I *was* able to narrow the number of possible sites to 25. That's after eliminating the open-pit mines and assuming that the mine we're looking for is located in the southern half of the state."

"Open-pit mines?"

"Basically, big holes in the ground."

"The hole we saw in those pictures is definitely in the side of a mountain."

Twenty-five mines meant that there still would be a lot of ground to cover; nevertheless, 25 would be a lot easier to deal with than 125. I tried to keep my voice light. "Can you map out a route for us?"

"By us, I'm assuming you mean you and me?"

"You hardly ever take a day off, Terry. We could check out at least a few of the closest ones."

"I'll try to check out the mine locations today, but I doubt whether I'll be able to get time off tomorrow. It's pretty short notice, and we're pretty busy around here."

"Well, give it a try anyway. Any news about the case?"

"Anthony Hunter was released from jail this morning. The D.A. ruled there was insufficient evidence to charge him with murder."

"Staatz warned me that would happen. What about Imfeldt's suicide…has anything new turned up there?"

"Not yet. All the Scottsdale PD will say is that preliminary interviews are underway."

The moment I hung up, it dawned on me that, of course, the mine we were looking for would likely be somewhere near Imfeldt's cotton fields. Using that additional criterion, Terry might be able to narrow our "mine field" down even further. I was just about to punch in his number when the phone rang again. This time, no name appeared in the window. I stared at the unfamiliar number, silently commanding it to disappear and the ringing to cease. Voice mail kicked in, and a voice tinged with no small degree of aggravation said, "This is Roberto Guzman, Jeff's academic counselor. I've been trying to reach him for several days. Please have him give me a call at his earliest convenience."

I punched in Jeff's number, and he picked up immediately.

"Your academic counselor just called here looking for you. Haven't you been answering your phone?"

"It's no big deal, Mom. I just don't feel like talking to him right now."

"Jeff, I know that the past few weeks have been rough. Haven't you been going to your classes? Is that what he's calling about?"

There was a long pause. "No. I mean, no, I haven't been going to class and yes, that's probably what he's calling about. I'm sorry."

"If you need time off from school, why not take a semester's leave? Start fresh in August?"

"If I did, I wouldn't be able to stay in the dorms...and I wouldn't be able to graduate in May."

"I happen to think that December graduations are quite festive. And you can stay here with us for a while."

"Is that allowed? I thought Sun Lakes had a rule that only old people could live there."

"I'll ignore that remark," I said. "I'll get special dispensation, or whatever...I'm sure it will be all right. I mean, it's not like you're moving in permanently."

"Do you have enough room for me to store my stuff for a while?"

"We'll make room."

"And my aquarium?"

"No problem."

I called Terry to give him the news. While he wasn't exactly ecstatic about it at first, he quickly warmed to the idea and even offered to move my work station to his study so that Jeff could have the guest room to himself and I could work uninterrupted by the strains of techno rock.

I asked him if he'd be able to find out if any of the 25 mines were on or close to Imfeldt's cotton farm. "Good call. I'm just putting together some stuff for the noon show, and I'll take a look at Imfeldt's land…if there's a mine entrance anywhere on it, Google Earth will find it."

I spent the next two hours readying the guest room for Jeff, including clearing out the extra stacks of linens I'd just arranged on the closet shelf. Moving out my desk and computer would have to wait for some additional muscle power and technological know-how, i.e., the Winters men. I'd just stretched out on the sofa for an afternoon power nap when the phone rang again. It was Terry, and his voice was much more energized than it had been during our last conversation.

"Good news!" he said.

"You found something?"

"There's no mine near Imfeldt's cotton fields."

I groaned. "Then why are you so happy?"

"Because there *is* one on twenty acres of land he owns near Jerome. But we'll have to take a drive up there Saturday. No way can I do it tomorrow."

"Terry, I don't think I can wait that long…and I do happen to know someone who might like to take a nice drive in the country."

Chapter Eighteen
Wednesday

Despite Terry's objections and my grudging promise not to do any spelunking without him (I had my fingers crossed behind my back), Aunt Sally picked me up at six a.m., and we headed out Riggs to the 1-10. The interstate would take us to the 17 and north to Jerome, a historic mining town nestled in the Black Hills of Yavapai County. Its population is tiny and its tourist trade huge, largely due to breathtaking 360-degree views of the Verde Valley, which are accessible from a height of five thousand feet above sea level, and its creepy-fun reputation for multiple-site hauntings.

I felt a pang of guilt at not being home to help Terry get Jeff settled in, but I'd left a note on the kitchen counter to remind them that there was baked ham and homemade mac and cheese in the fridge. I'd learned from my mom at an early age that comfort food makes the best peace offering for all kinds of sins and slights, real or imagined.

We stopped in Prescott for breakfast at an old-fashioned diner before continuing to Jerome, which the town website proudly refers to as "America's Most Vertical City," and the "Largest Ghost Town in America." Twenty minutes later, Aunt Sally was maneuvering Arnold up the thirty-degree mountain incline that led to the town proper. Looming ahead was the famed Jerome Grand Hotel, its resident ghosts proving more of a tourist draw than its hospitality or amenities. The formidable structure sat atop a hill like an aging queen looking down on her subjects from a lofty throne. Terry and I had once stayed at the hotel, in a top-floor room with a spectacular view, and had been awakened at two a.m. by the unmistakable sound of invisible coins being dropped, one by one, into the old claw-foot tub in the bathroom. I'm sure we'd have fallen back to sleep had it not been for the ghostly whispers that emanated from the empty space around our bed for the remainder of the night.

We drove west into the foothills. Imfeldt's country home (his primary residence was in Scottsdale), located a few miles north of town, was an elegant stucco hacienda that looked to be about five thousand square feet. It had a pillared portico on three sides, a detached casita that was a miniature replica of the main house, and a drive encircling a stone fountain that featured three life-size peasant girls emptying pails of water into a massive basin. Imfeldt's heirs would no doubt be fighting over this little gem of a property.

We parked in the middle of a cluster of pine trees that separated a stretch of manicured lawn from the road. The sweet, woodsy fragrance that surrounded us as we emerged from the car somewhat atoned for the fact that Terry and I had skipped the tree that Christmas. Aunt Sally, purse suspended from an arm, made a beeline for the house.

"Aunt Sally, wait a minute. What if someone's home?"

"The old guy's dead. If anyone's home, it would be a spider or two and maybe a few flies dumb enough to get caught in their web."

We reached the front portico and, mesmerized by its grandeur, slowly made our way up the stairs. A line of six filigree wrought-iron chandeliers graced the high ceiling; matching sconces adorned either side of the varnished walnut double doors that served as the main entrance.

I walked up to one of the tall front windows, but heavy drapes had been drawn closed to prevent anyone from seeing inside. I looked back toward Arnold, the only car within view, and took in the scene around us. Apparently, as Aunt Sally had predicted, no one was home.

After we finished a cursory walk-through of the property, including the back patio overlooking a swimming pool (complete with waterfall and spa) and the casita, also locked up tighter than a drum, we headed back to the car, stopping briefly to peer through windows on each side of doors set into a barn that had been converted into a garage. The interior was unlighted, but the natural light from the windows was sufficient to reveal a line of stalls that housed classic cars representing a variety of years and models. A Caterpillar equipped with a large front blade blocked the stall closest to the front door.

"I wish Terry was here. He'd love to get a look at these cars."

The sound of footsteps crunched on the gravel drive behind us. "Uh-oh. Looks like we got company," said Aunt Sally.

I turned to see a man who looked as if he were on his way to herd cattle or lasso some steers, or maybe audition to be an extra in a Western, if they made Westerns anymore. He was perfectly polished and groomed, from the top of his Stetson to the toes of his Luccheses, and his grin revealed teeth that could have landed him a role in a toothpaste commercial. "Excuse me, ladies, may I be of some assistance to y'all? I'm Stevie Bryce."

Steven Bryce, the attorney who'd gone ballistic when Dieter Imfeldt had been removed from his client list and given to Tom. I was unable to suppress a sharp intake of breath, which garnered a curious look from Bryce.

His blue eyes squinting against the afternoon sun, Bryce looked us over. "May I be so bold as to ask your names?"

"I'm Amanda…Smith, and this is my Aunt Sally," I said.

Bryce nodded and folded his arms in front of him. "This here is private property," he said. "If y'all are lookin' for a place to stay for the night, you might want to try the Grand Hotel in Jerome. If you're easily spooked by ghosts and you've a mind to drive a few more miles to the southeast, Prescott's got some nice hotels."

Aunt Sally was flustered, and, never one to weigh her words, started right in. "Oh no, we were…"

"…wondering if this property had been put up for sale yet," I finished after pushing my way in front of her. "We heard about Mr. Imfeldt's untimely death. So sad. He must have been horribly depressed to have taken his own life."

"Yes, ma'am, a terrible tragedy it was." Bryce studied us with bemusement before turning his head to take a better look at Aunt Sally's old Cadillac parked at the side of the road. "You say you're interested in purchasing *this* here property?"

"Who wouldn't be?" I beamed, and extended an arm toward the house.

"Well, you're a little ahead of the game," he said. "In fact, as Mr. Imfeldt's attorney, I just met with his farm manager and a few of the family members to discuss the disposition of the estate. But I'm sure that when the place hits the market, you'll know about it soon enough."

I looked over Bryce's shoulder toward the house. "Is any of the family at home?" I asked. "We'd like to express our condolences." I really would have loved the chance to see the inside of that house and maybe get a bit more information about Imfeldt's supposed suicide.

"No, ma'am. Everyone's gone except a few of the house staff. But I'll surely pass your kind words along to the family next chance I get."

"We'd better get going, Aunt Sally." I offered a hand to Bryce. "Thank you so much for your time."

"My pleasure, Ms.—Smith, was it?"

"That's right," I said, taking Aunt Sally's arm. "And thanks again."

When we reached Arnold, I turned around to see that Bryce was still watching us. I gave him a cheerful wave before getting into the car. "Let's get Arnold cranked up and move on."

"Why don't you take a breath and relax," said Aunt Sally. "It's not like we broke any laws. I mean, the gate was wide open."

"I know, but I didn't want Cowboy Joe, there, to ask any more questions."

"Do you have any idea how to get to the mine from here?" asked Aunt Sally. She leaned over me to pull a map from the glove compartment. "Take a look at this, will you? And where are we going to have lunch? Esther and her son were here a few months ago, and she said they have some good restaurants."

"Is it all right if we do lunch after the mine?" I said. "I'm kind of anxious to get this over with."

Ten minutes later, I told Aunt Sally to pull off the road. We parked in the area that, according to Terry's directions, was within half a mile of the mine entrance. I left Aunt Sally to rest on a large, flat rock shaded by a large cottonwood tree and hiked deeper into the foothills until I spotted the mine entrance. Judging from the surrounding landscape, it had to be the one in Tom's photos. The only difference was the presence of several huge boulders that now partially blocked the opening. Just to be safe, I marked the path back to Arnold by breaking branches as I moved through the scrub. I retrieved Aunt Sally, and we took a slow but steady walk back to the mine, finally reaching the entrance.

"We're not actually going in there, are we?" Aunt Sally's voice wavered. "I don't think anyone's been through that door for a hundred years. It's almost completely blocked by those rocks."

"I'm sure it's safe, Aunt Sally. Look...it's not that old. You can still see the rails." I gazed up at the top of the hill. "There must have been a landslide since the satellite's last pass. The entrance was wide open in the Google Earth photo Terry and I were looking at last night."

"Maybe someone put those rocks there on purpose," said Aunt Sally. "Maybe someone used that Caterpillar inside Imfeldt's garage to put those rocks there—you know, to keep anyone from poking around in that mine."

"All the more reason for us to go in and take a look around," I said, examining a narrow opening between two large boulders. "Do you think there's enough room for us to squeeze through?"

We discovered that the opening was so narrow that we literally did have to squeeze through. "Thank God for Weight Watchers," quipped Aunt Sally.

Inside, once we got a few yards beyond the entrance, it was as dark as...well, as the inside of a cave. My inner Girl Scout showing, I'd remembered to bring a sturdy flashlight, while Aunt Sally had brought a couple of four-inch pink metallic cheapies she'd purchased at the hardware store. She now held one of the mini-flashlights in each hand and directed their feeble beams toward the walls of the mine.

"Keep close," I said, and led the way along the rails into the mine tunnel. The deeper we went, the narrower the tunnel grew. Metal-caged Edison lights had been strung along the damp walls, but given the thick covering of dust and rust, they obviously hadn't been used in decades.

"Do you think there are any bats in here?" I'd heard a muffled squeaking, and I was pretty sure it wasn't coming from my Keds.

"They won't hurt you if you don't hurt them," said Aunt Sally. "We had bats in the attic when I was a kid."

"Right."

The rock ceiling above us suddenly got a whole lot lower, and I was glad that claustrophobia wasn't in my Cluster C repertoire. Every 15 feet or so, rough-hewn logs had been jammed in upright positions to stabilize the sides and ceiling of the mine. Thankfully, it wasn't too much longer before the path widened and the ceiling became taller again. I directed my flashlight into the distance ahead, and its beam was swallowed up in the darkness of a large cavern. I danced the light up and around the entrance to the area to reveal a large "PRIVATE PROPERTY—KEEP OUT" sign.

I started to move forward into the cavern, but Aunt Sally grabbed hold of my sleeve and pulled me back. "Hold on."

"What? You don't seriously believe we should pay attention to those signs!"

"This place gives me the creeps. Maybe we should come back later with Terry…and a few of his friends."

"Do you want to go back and wait for me at the car?"

There was a pause, and I knew she was considering the offer. Then finally, "No. I'm not leaving you alone. But let's hurry it up, okay?"

We slowly continued our way through the darkness until we stood in the center of the huge chamber. Water dripped from the ceiling above us, and the temperature had abruptly dropped a good ten degrees.

I shivered and stepped closer to Aunt Sally. "Can you see anything?"

She shone her two narrow beams up and across the considerable expanse of rock wall.

"Wait a minute...I think I do," she said, following her two tiny beams to a smaller wall of rock that jutted out into the cavernous space. "There's another room back here."

I made my way to where Aunt Sally stood and focused my flashlight into the darkness in front of us. "Oh, my God."

Someone had used the rear cavern as a dumping ground for drums like the ones in Tom's photos. Rust covered much of their surface, but on a few of the barrels, some of the red paint was still discernable: "1997" and "VENENO."

"There must be at least a hundred barrels in here," said Aunt Sally.

"Hand me your cell phone, will you? I want to get some pictures."

Aunt Sally gave me a quick lesson on cell phone photography. "You really need to step up into the twenty-first century, Amanda."

I ignored the barb. "Just take my flashlight and aim it at those drums."

After taking some shots from various angles, I tried to call Terry. No matter where I stood or how high I held the phone, however, I couldn't get a signal.

"What's wrong?" asked Aunt Sally, her face reflecting eerily in the blackness.

"I'll have to call from outside," I said. "And I'd better phone Staatz before I call Terry. He'll be interested to know what we found and how we came to find it."

"I don't think Staatz is going to be happy to find out that we're snooping around on our own," said Aunt Sally.

"We have to tell him—we don't have a choice. Let's just hope he won't arrest me for withholding evidence…again."

I could actually hear Aunt Sally's teeth chattering now. "I need to get out of here," she said. "This place feels like a tomb." A large drop of water fell onto the lens of her glasses. "Where's all that cold water coming from?" she asked, and wiped her glasses with a handkerchief.

"It must be seepage from the ground above," I said. "The water acts like an air-conditioning system. That's why it's so cold in here."

I handed Aunt Sally's phone back to her. "Well, I guess we found what we were looking for. Here, put the phone back in your purse till we're outside."

We turned to head back to the mine entrance and had almost reached it, when there was a loud rumbling, and the little bit of light that had been filtering in through the opening vanished in a cloud of dust.

Chapter Nineteen

Aunt Sally directed her flashlights at what used to be the mine entrance. "What just happened?!"

"A landslide." My voice was thick with fear. "Hand me your phone again. I want to try and get a signal."

After Aunt Sally fished the phone from her purse and passed it to me, I climbed to the top of one of the boulders that had fallen so that half of it lay outside the mine, while the other half lay inside. I held the phone at arm's length, standing on tiptoes and stretching as far as I could. "Still no signal."

With a heavy sigh, I sat down on the rock and propped an elbow on my knee, using it as a brace to reinforce my hold on the heavy flashlight. "If you ask me, this is no coincidence. Remember that Caterpillar we saw parked inside Imfeldt's garage? Someone would easily be able to start a landslide with that thing."

"Do you think Bryce got suspicious and followed us here?"

"That thought has crossed my mind," I said. "We can think about the whos, whys, and hows later." I brushed rock dust from the front of my pants and studied the space around us. "Right now, we have to find another way out of here. Even if we had something to dig with, there's no way we'd be able to leave the same way we came in. I'm assuming that's a solid wall of rock blocking the entrance now."

"Can you remember if there were any other holes in the side of the mountain?" Aunt Sally asked hopefully.

"I didn't see any on Google Earth, but that doesn't necessarily mean they're not there." My stomach rumbled, and the sound seemed comically exaggerated in the stillness of the mine. "Now I wish I'd listened to you about having lunch before coming here."

"Not to worry," said Aunt Sally. She slid her handbag from her shoulder and shone her mini-lights into its interior. "I still got one Danish in here…as long as you don't mind that it looks more like a pancake…you know, from when you sat on me the other day." She dug into the bottom of the purse. "And I got half a box of cough drops. That's it."

"I have a full bottle of water in my bag," I said. "It should last us a while, but I think we'd better hold off as long as we can. That Danish may be today's lunch and dinner, and maybe even tomorrow's breakfast…we don't know how long it'll take us to find a way out."

"If there *is* a way out to find," Aunt Sally added. "And we can have the cough drops for dessert. They're the chewy, cherry kind."

We started back toward the chamber where the drums holding what we assumed to be DDT were stashed. To save time, we decided to separate: Aunt Sally took a path to the left, close to one wall of the chamber, and I moved slowly through the center of the room and the expanse of barrels, many of which had been overturned. My flashlight didn't expose any leaks, and I didn't smell anything except mustiness, yet I couldn't help but wonder if I'd be glowing green once I made it to the other side of the sea of toxic drums. As I stepped on and around the drums, I wondered what else could possibly happen that already hadn't: one murder victim, Nathan, and two more likely victims, Tom Reynolds and Dieter Imfeldt; the apartment trashing; Anthony Hunter's arrest and subsequent release; Dinah's garage break-in and her attempted suicide;

Jeff's attack on Aaron; and now this…my mind reeled, thoughts streaming through my consciousness like a high-speed train with no brakes.

With only my flashlight to guide my way, it wasn't long before I became disoriented. The darkness around me dissolved into amorphous shapes that zigzagged toward me and, just when they seemed to be close enough to touch, melted away before reappearing in different places. Waves of nausea hit me with sudden force, and I latched onto one of the rusty drums, clinging to it the same way a weak swimmer clings to a piece of flotsam to keep from going under. The worst of the waves passed, and the sounds of Aunt Sally's footfalls echoing faintly through the chamber broke through the murkiness to restore my sense of time and space. Something skittered across the path directly in front of me; I couldn't see it, but I definitely heard it. Whatever it was, it was large enough for its footsteps to be audible. They were louder, in fact, than Aunt Sally's.

My words could have come right off the page of some B horror movie script. "Something's in here with us!"

"Probably just a spider. I've noticed a few." Aunt Sally's voice was inordinately calm, which meant that she was at the point of saying anything to keep me from going over the edge. Unbeknownst to her, I was already over it and hanging on by a thread. "Are you all right, Amanda?"

"Yes," I said through clenched teeth. The panic attack had struck with force but already seemed to be running out of steam. Another one might follow on its heels, but at least for the moment, my breathing and heart rate had returned to nearly normal.

"Want to switch places for a while?" asked Aunt Sally.

"No, I'll be all right. I think I'm almost to the far wall. My voice seems to be bouncing back to me pretty fast now."

"I don't see anything on my side," said Aunt Sally. "No light, no hole… nothing. Do you—"

The sound of my cry as my toe made contact with solid rock cut off the rest of her sentence.

Her voice echoed from the far end of the chamber. "Are you okay?!"

"I think so. I walked into a wall, but at least my toe found it before my nose did." I swept the length of the rock wall with my light. "I think I see another tunnel back here."

"Wait right there," said Aunt Sally. "I'm coming over. Don't move."

We aimed our lights into the tunnel, which looked to be about 12 feet wide. Since our pooled light penetrated only about twenty feet into the solid blackness, I couldn't even guess at the tunnel's depth. That part of the ground our light could reach glimmered white with a chalky dust, but rocks and pieces of lumber had fallen or been strewn along the path, making it difficult to navigate. We were ready for a break only 15 minutes in and chose a decaying beam to serve as our combination picnic table/bench. Aunt Sally tore off a small piece of the Danish for each of us, and I passed the water to her after taking a tiny sip. A feast it wasn't, but Danish and water had never tasted so good. Hydrated and somewhat fed, we plodded ahead with a newfound attitude of resoluteness.

And then a cool wisp of air touched my cheek. "Either this mine is haunted, or that's air coming from somewhere up ahead," I said.

"I can feel it, too," said Aunt Sally.

Our light bobbed and weaved through the darkness ahead. "It must be an opening of some kind," I said.

It was an opening, but nothing larger than a mouse would have been able to get through it. Dejected, I sat down and buried my face in my hands. The ground I was sitting on was uneven and, to my discomfort, swelled to form a hard, mesa-like top layer that crested right at the point where it met my bottom.

"What the heck am I sitting on?!" I exclaimed, and jumped to my feet.

Aunt Sally bent over and peered down at the ground where I'd been sitting. "I hope I'm wrong, but I'm pretty sure it's a grave."

Chapter Twenty

Aunt Sally, clutching my arm so tightly that it threatened to stop my blood flow, asked, "Who do you think it is?"

"I have no idea," I said, all the while thinking that it could very well be Tom Reynolds. I gently detached her hand from my arm and led her away from the mound of packed earth to a rock that offered an Aunt Sally-sized ledge. "Aunt Sally, sit here near the air flow and rest a while. I've got an idea."

"I hope it's a good one."

"I'm going to try and find something I can use to make that opening bigger."

"It would take forever to make it big enough for one of us to get through," she said. "Even me. We'll both starve to death first."

I moved close to the wall, directed the flashlight's beam on the area surrounding the opening, and studied it closely as I moved my free palm along the wall's rough surface.

"This must have been an emergency exit at one time." I stood on a rock that put me at face level with the opening and peered into it. "The miners either closed it up, or another landslide blocked it."

"How much rock do you think is out there?" asked Aunt Sally.

"I don't know, but I can see light through this hole, so right here it's shallow enough for me to be able to make it a little bigger—at least enough to get my arm through to the outside. If I can do that, I might be able to get a signal on your phone."

"One of those timbers we saw back at the entrance to the tunnel might work. You could use it as a battering ram."

"I'll go take a look." I handed the water bottle to Aunt Sally. "Don't move from that rock, and make sure you stay hydrated."

"All right, but I wish I'd thought to bring my flask. I could use a nip right now."

As I set out to find a suitable beam—one that hadn't gone soft with decay—I considered what the implications would be if the mound of earth in the mine's rear chamber actually was a grave, more specifically Tom Reynold's grave. The fact was, I had a strong feeling that it was a grave and that Tom's remains lay under that mound.

I thought of Dinah. Nathan had been murdered less than two weeks ago. Dinah had gone through the agony of identifying her son's body, selecting a casket whose gleaming finish he would never admire, ordering flowers whose fragrance he would never enjoy, making arrangements with the church's ladies guild for food and drink he would never taste. Now she faced the prospect of going through the ordeal again, with barely enough time to breathe, let alone heal. Up to this point, the possibility that Tom had been murdered a decade earlier had been merely a theory, a hypothesis that had no physical proof to confirm it one way or the other. A grave with physical remains would prove the hypothesis; bones and DNA would turn the theory into fact. Even if Tom had been dead and buried in this mine for ten years, Dinah would be experiencing his death now, in the present. And she would have to begin the grieving process all over again.

As I made my way along the path to the front entrance, I moved my beam from side to side in search of something I could use as a battering ram and spotted a number of three-foot poles, many with a circumference of about six inches. For the first time since we'd been trapped, I felt hope.

Back in the rear chamber, I said, "There was a pile of these things back there. This one matches the poles they used for cross-braces along the walls inside the adit, so it should be pretty sturdy." I rested one end of the pole on the ground and tilted the other end toward Aunt Sally. "Do me a favor and hang onto this until I get up onto that rock." I set the flashlight down and said, "When I get a good foothold, hand me the pole and keep the flashlight aimed at that opening."

"You got it."

I crawled up onto the rock, which was shaped like a steep, two-step staircase, and reached out for the pole. I held it steady and straight, like a javelin, with both hands encircling it, and forced its pointed end into the opening with a hard jab. Small bits of rock crumbled into dust, but the size of the opening looked exactly the same. I repeated the process, and each time the pole struck the rock edge, a tiny bit more of it crumbled, leaving the opening essentially unchanged. After only ten minutes, the force of the jabs diminished, and I was definitely beginning to tire.

"Why not let me give it a try?" asked Aunt Sally.

"Even if you could get up here, you'd never be able to reach that hole. You're too short."

I repositioned myself so that I was closer to the opening and, using shorter jabs, attacked the hole again. On the third jab, a large chunk of rock came loose.

Aunt Sally jumped to her feet. "How the heck did you do that?!"

"Prayer, and a bit of luck. Hand me the cell." Phone in hand, I pushed my arm through the opening to see how far it would go.

"My hand's outside, and boy, does that air feel good." My goal was to key in 9-1-1, push my arm through the opening, and hopefully, press "send" on the phone's tiny screen. The trouble was, I couldn't see my hand and therefore couldn't see where my finger was placed on the screen. I pressed what I thought might be "send" and waited for several minutes before pulling the phone back in to see if I'd struck gold. On the third try, I said, "I think I've got it this time…"

Turning to Aunt Sally with a confident smile, I immediately lost my footing on the rock. My body floundered, my left arm waving wildly in the air, my right arm somehow maintaining its position inside the opening. I knew that I was about to fall, so I half-jumped from the rock while at the same time pulling my arm sharply back toward me and withdrawing it from the hole.

"Whew!" exclaimed Aunt Sally. "That was a close one," Then, "Hey, where's my phone?"

I stared at my hand as though it belonged to a stranger and said, "I dropped it. I lost it—I just threw away our only hope of getting out of here."

Chapter Twenty-One

I felt absolutely miserable and completely responsible for the situation I'd gotten us into. Not only had I dropped the phone outside the hole, it was my bright idea to try and find Imfeldt's mine in the first place. I sat down on the ground next to Aunt Sally's rock and muttered, "Well, there goes that idea." To keep from bursting into tears, I forced a dry laugh. I propped the flashlight against the rock's edge. The light was now a lantern that illuminated the chamber in a cozy glow that reminded me of the days when Terry and I used to camp out with Jeff.

Aunt Sally, her short legs barely touching the ground, leaned toward the light as though seeking the warmth of a fire and sighed. "We still might have a chance: If you managed to hit 'send' before you dropped the phone, someone might be able to track us through the GPS."

"Maybe." I asked her to bring out the Danish remnants. "This just might be our last supper." I immediately regretted saying it. "Sorry. That wasn't funny." But I got no arguments…only two sad eyes peering at me through thick lenses.

Aunt Sally painstakingly counted out three small pieces of Danish for each of us and folded the rest back up in the napkin before returning it to her purse. I placed one small piece in my mouth and made it last as long as I could.

"If you did get through to 9-1-1, how long before emergency services gets here, do you think? I mean, I don't want to put the kibosh on this party, but considering our food and water supplies, I figure we have a day before we…you know."

I knew all too well but made a point of not reacting to her grim prediction. "I guess it depends on how many cell towers there are in the area. The more towers, the more accurately they'll be able to pinpoint our location." I tossed back the last of my Danish before continuing. "That's assuming, of course, that I did get through to 9-1-1, and that the operator didn't come to the conclusion that someone misdialed or that some kids were playing around."

"What about the mountains?" Aunt Sally asked. "Would they block the signal?"

"I don't think so. We're pretty high up here." I turned to her, my face brightening with an epiphany. "Terry and Jeff know that we're here. When we don't come home tonight, they'll call the authorities. We just have to hang in there a little while longer."

"I hate to say it, but Terry and Jeff probably won't miss you until the food runs out."

"They'll come for us soon," I said. I hugged my arms and glanced toward the mound of earth that I suspected was Tom Reynold's grave. "They have to."

I silently added, *but they won't be able to identify us without dental records. Maybe we should just give in and start digging two more graves right now.*

I passed the water bottle to Aunt Sally again. "Just a sip." There was enough left for us to have almost two ounces each. We spent the next hour telling stories and reminiscing about my dad. Aunt Sally had plenty of stories to share, like the time she was 14 and Dad was 18, and he locked her in her closet one night because he didn't trust the guy that was coming to pick her up for a drive-in movie date. She actually got me to laugh, there, for a minute.

Giddy with fatigue, we decided to call it a night. We needed to rest. Using our handbags as pillows, we tried to fool our bodies into thinking they were comfortable enough to sleep. Despite our less than cozy accommodations, Aunt Sally had no trouble falling asleep and began to snore softly. When the snoring seemed to become increasingly louder—alarmingly so––I realized that what I was hearing was the sound of rotor blades.

"Aunt Sally, wake up! I hear a helicopter!"

I jumped up onto the rock step and peered through the hole. "I can't see a thing—it's still pitch black out there."

Aunt Sally picked up the pole I'd used to enlarge the opening. "Here—use my handkerchief as a flag and wave it around out there."

She held the flashlight while I inserted the pole into the opening, pushing it through as far as it would go. I jerked it back and forth, and sideways…hopefully, someone in that helicopter would notice.

The sound of the rotors grew deafening, and we knew that our SOS had been seen: The helicopter was landing. Ten minutes later, the sweet, gruff sound of a man's voice came through the opening loud and clear. "Hold on! We've got rescue equipment on the way."

The man asked how many we were, and our names. Before too long, two bottles of water and two granola bars were pushed in through the opening, along with Aunt Sally's phone. When the rescue crew came, they told us to return to the mine entrance, where a bulldozer was already at work clearing the rockfall. "There's not enough room on this side to bring in the equipment."

"You'd better get the local law enforcement out here," I called through the opening. "We found a hundred or so drums that we suspect contain DDT. And we also may have found a body."

The Jerome PD put us up in a bed and breakfast for the night…nothing fancy, but it was clean, and the bed was soft and comfortable. I called Terry to let him know what had happened. He was so happy to hear that we were all right, he barely scolded me at all for the bad judgment I showed by going inside the mine and taking Aunt Sally along for the ride.

"You were supposed to be on a scouting mission to find the mine. You were supposed to wait until I could go in there with you…you were supposed to…"

"I know, but we're fine. And I found what I was looking for. Terry. Those drums of DDT are still in that mine. And I think we may have found Tom."

"What are you saying?"

"Don't mention anything to Dinah yet, but we found a grave inside the mine."

"I want you home right now."

"Tomorrow. Right now, we're going to try and get a few hours of sleep."

*****

After breakfast the next day, we stopped at the police station, a tan stucco building attached to the Jerome Town Hall, a structure dating back to the turn of the twentieth century. The streets of America's largest ghost town teemed with tourists, many of whom had traveled from Europe and Asia, stopping on their way to Las Vegas or Disneyland to get a glimpse of the old—but no longer all that wild—West.

Sergeant Norman Farwell, a jovial middle-aged man with a white handlebar moustache, confirmed our fears that the mound of earth we'd slept next to the night before was, indeed, a grave.

"We'll be sending the remains to the county medical examiner over in Prescott."

Aunt Sally's face blanched, and I knew that she was able to stand only because I had a firm arm around her waist.

"Do you know who it is?" she asked, her voice tremulous.

"Now, that's something I couldn't rightly tell you at this time, ma'am." He studied her with concern and pulled out one of two chairs from a small, round table in the corner of the office. "You better sit down here for a bit."

"We think that someone may have started that landslide on purpose," I said.

Farwell studied me with skepticism. "You don't say?"

"We saw a Caterpillar equipped with a shovel blade in Dieter Imfeldt's garage. I think someone may have followed us to the mine and used it to block the entrance while we were inside."

Farwell picked up the phone on his desk and punched in some numbers. "Frankie boy...are you anywhere near the Imfeldt place? Good, good. Do me a favor and check out the garage. I'm particularly interested in a Caterpillar with a blade attachment. Get some samples of whatever's on that blade and bring 'em in to the office."

He set down the phone and folded his hands on the desk in front of him. "Mind if I ask you ladies what you were doing poking around Imfeldt's garage? Did you know the man passed on a few days ago? The family's going through a hard time right now. I expect they don't need strangers roaming around the property and meddling in their business."

I glanced at Aunt Sally, who responded with a "you're on your own," look before focusing on the rotating blades of the ceiling fan above her head.

"We were in the area and decided on impulse to take a peek...and the gate was open."

Sergeant Farwell rocked back in his chair. "Tell me, what business brought you to that old copper mine in the first place?"

"We were looking for the drums in these photos." I rummaged in my purse and pulled out the slim box containing Tom's pictures. "And as you know, we found them."

Farwell studied each of the photos with interest. "I had a feeling there'd be more to this story than meets the eye."

"You'll want to call Detective Roy Staatz with the Tempe PD," I said. "The body and the drums we found inside that mine are probably related to a case he's working on."

Farwell nodded thoughtfully. "I will do that, ma'am."

"It's possible that those remains belong to a man named Tom Reynolds. He disappeared ten years ago. Detective Staatz can provide whatever information you need to make a positive ID."

Farwell smoothed his moustache with thumbs and forefingers. "If Reynolds disappeared a decade ago, why all the interest now?"

"His son was murdered a week ago, and we think his murder is somehow connected to his father's disappearance."

The drive back was subdued. "I need to get home. There's a bottle of brandy there with my name on it," said Aunt Sally.

"Are you going to be all right?"

"I didn't last this long for no good reason. I'll be fine—as long as you don't get me into any more trouble."

It was nearly noon when we pulled into Sun Lakes. Aunt Sally's cell phone rang; she answered it and listened briefly before handing it to me. "It's that detective guy. He wants to talk to you."

My hand was shaking as I accepted the phone. I knew I'd crossed the line by not handing over Tom's photos right away. And now, I was about to pay the price.

"This is Amanda."

"I'm returning your call, Mrs. Winters."

I'd completely forgotten I'd left Staatz a message before leaving for Jerome yesterday morning. It seemed as though a week, rather than just a day, had passed since then; being trapped inside a mine for 24 hours does strange things to one's sense of time and space. I told Staatz about me and Dinah nearly being run off the road the other night by a black pickup truck...the same kind of truck Aaron Hunter drove. "What time did Aaron leave the station the night before last?" I asked.

"Shortly after you did, but there's no way he could have been the one watching Mrs. Reynold's house...unless he split himself in two and sent one half to Ocotillo Springs while the other was here in Tempe filing a complaint against your son."

"You're right about that, but he had plenty of time to get over to Dinah's house later and follow us to Sun Lakes."

Staatz didn't respond to that. He said that his request for 24-hour security for Dinah had been denied. "There just wasn't enough support for it, and the department's budget is tight right now." He added, however, that beginning the next day, a squad would be doing hourly patrols past her house.

I started to tell him about our discoveries in the mine and the landslide, but he cut me off, his voice hardened. "Sergeant Farwell has already been in touch with me and told me the whole story. I need to have you turn over those photos as evidence, Mrs. Winters. I'm growing a bit tired of this. First your son with those emails, and now you, with these photographs. Do I need to explain one more time what obstruction of justice means, and what the consequences are?"

"No," I said, humbly receiving my comeuppance from the detective yet again. "Has anything come back on those remains?"

"No, no…we won't have an ID for a few weeks yet. We're talking Prescott, here, not Phoenix, but even under the best of conditions, DNA testing is usually a long, drawn-out process. Anyway, Farwell's team checked out Imfeldt's garage. They found the Caterpillar you mentioned…soil samples from the shovel blade are already on the way to the lab for testing. But they found something else in that garage."

"What?"

"A '75 royal blue Triumph in mint condition."

Chapter Twenty-Two

It was Tom's Triumph, of course.

I thought about how Staatz would break the news to Dinah, and what I would say to her. I told myself that she'd be all right. Some experts on the subject say that it's better to give bad news all at once—just get it over and done with—but I think exactly the opposite is true. I'd much rather get bad news bit by bit rather than being propelled head-first into the whole, horrible mess of it.

Dinah had been hurled, screaming and kicking, into her bad news...her horrific news. There had been no luxury of a warning...no soft-pedaling in the interest of shock protection: *Mrs. Reynolds, your son was found dead, drowned in the Salt River, a gunshot wound to the head.*

But that wasn't to be the end of it. If that hadn't been enough, another bit surfaced: *Despite the impression you've been under for the past ten years, your husband may not have abandoned you and your son after all: He may have been murdered.*

I had to help my friend...do whatever was necessary to see her through this nightmare, Cluster C be damned.

The house was empty when Aunt Sally dropped me off. I poured myself a glass of wine and took it out to the patio, where I closed my eyes and let my thoughts run their course. One theory seemed very plausible, and very simple: *Aaron Hunter killed Tom in retaliation for his mother's death—murder by DDT. When the opportunity to get rid of Nathan cropped up ten years later, he took advantage of it. Then came the final coup: Imfeldt's so-called suicide.*

A second theory, seeming to make sense and to not make sense at the same time, nagged at me: *Dieter Imfeldt murdered Tom to keep him from presenting evidence at the tribal hearings...evidence that could potentially decimate both his business and, consequently, his wealth.* This theory was also plausible...but not so simple: Aside from the potential law suits, I'd read that federal fines for using banned pesticides were imposed in proportion to the value of the offending business. Given the value of Imfeldt's business, the fines would be staggering. However, although I could buy the idea of Imfeldt killing Tom ten years ago to keep those photos from surfacing, I still couldn't quite believe that he'd arranged to meet Nathan, murdered him in cold blood, and then committed suicide out of remorse: A person committing murder at age 73 was somehow more believable than a person committing murder at age 83.

Maybe it was naïveté on my part. But I still couldn't accept the idea of a man like Imfeldt committing suicide...willingly giving up his picture-perfect life in this world—regardless of how many years of that life remained—for an uncertain one in the next.

Yet another theory, this one weak and sketchy, darted in and out of my thoughts. *Steven Bryce, a man known to have a temper, and who had become enraged when a lucrative client had been taken from him, murdered Tom out of pure jealousy.* The murder, had Bryce committed it, would also have served as the first step in clearing a path to his most recent role as Imfeldt's attorney, the role held previously by Tom.

Bit: Remains that may once have been the husband and father known as Tom Reynolds were found in an abandoned copper mine on Imfeldt's property. Bit: Tom's '75 Triumph was found in Imfeldt's garage.

I heard the patio doors slide open, and Terry stepped out, gave me a kiss, and said, "I went to Bashas. I've got ham on rye, potato salad, and chips. Oh, and I picked up an extra cold bottle of Kendall Jackson for you and a six-pack of Corona for me."

I started to rise. "I can fix us some plates."

"I've got this. You just stay here and relax."

How I loved that man.

The warm weather was holding, and the pool was beginning to look inviting even to me. Come July, I'd have to invest in some noodles, goggles, and whatever other safety equipment I could find for my first round of swimming lessons. I wanted to conquer my fear of water. I wanted to be able to dip my toes into the pool without passing out and drowning. I gazed off into the distance, beyond the roofs of the houses across the street and over the canopies of tall palm trees edging Alma School Road, to watch three hot air balloons, one multicolor stripe and the other two a bright red, floating in a lazy procession above the San Tan peaks.

"I wonder what the mountains look like from up there." I pointed my sandwich toward the clouds, and Terry looked up to join me in watching the slow progress of the balloons as they glided across the sky.

"If I could ever get you up in a plane, you'd know what the mountains look like from up there. They're beautiful."

"Someday," I said. "I have to master the ground before I tackle the sky." The balloons disappeared from our view, and I asked, "Do you think you could get a day off from work?"

"That depends on what you've got in mind."

"How does a road trip to Mexico sound?"

"Mexico! But we're planning that trip to Vegas next month, and I..."

"I'm not talking vacation here. I'm talking a fact-finding mission...but as long as we're down there anyway, maybe lunch somewhere nice and a little shopping."

"What facts do you hope to find?"

"You said yourself that those drums came from Mexico. I found out that the production of DDT was banned in Mexico back in '97, but its use wasn't outlawed until 2000. We have to assume that the DDT was brought across the border sometime after that."

"And...?"

"And if we can find Imfeldt's DDT source, we might also be able to prove that he killed Tom, which would eliminate both Anthony and Aaron Hunter as suspects in Nathan's murder."

"Mexico is one heck of a big country, Amanda."

"I've been able to narrow things down to within 25 miles of Nogales. It shouldn't take us more than half a day to visit the factories."

There were several chemical plants that had manufactured DDT back in the eighties and nineties. After eliminating the big, international biotechs— Union Carbide, Dow, DuPont—the ones that wouldn't risk dumping the stuff illegally, I came up with three privately-owned Mexican plants that used to manufacture DDT and which were still in business.

Terry squeezed a lime slice into his beer. "Staatz would have us arrested if we bypassed him and took it upon ourselves to hunt down the source of that DDT. Can't you just make a few phone calls? Better yet, can't you just give the information to Staatz and let him deal with it?"

"Uh-uh. Staatz doesn't exactly keep me in the loop. I'd never know whether or not he really followed up on this. Besides, the passports we got for last year's trip to Puerto Peñasco are just moldering in my desk drawer. This trip is important to us, and to Dinah."

"We should at least turn over Tom's photos before we go."

"We can't, not yet. But I promise we will as soon as we get back. Please!"

My pleading worked, and Terry agreed to the trip. I called Dinah to see if she was interested. "I don't think so," she said. "Staatz called me about the grave...about Tom's Triumph. My parents have offered to let me stay with them in Tucson for a while, and I've decided to take them up on it. I just need to tie up a few things here before I leave...within the next few days."

"Dinah, I went to that mine hoping to find nothing more than those drums."

"I know, and I'm glad you thought to go there. If you hadn't, I might have never known what really happened to Tom."

"We don't know, yet, if it was him."

Dinah's voice was weak. "I do. I know."

Next, I called Aunt Sally. She must have been right on top of the phone because the first ring hadn't yet ended when she picked up.

"Amanda, I think I'm in love!"

"Are we talking Bernie here?"

"And how. But it's Ernie, not Bernie! He's an absolute living doll. He took me out for lunch at Applebee's. He's no cheapskate, either. I said we should order from the '2 for $20' menu...but he wouldn't hear of it. We're going to karaoke at the club Saturday night. I'm betting that man can croon like Crosby." She asked if I wanted to go back to Giovanni's for lunch the next day. "You missed a lot the last time, since you got sick and couldn't eat."

I begged off, and told her about the planned trip to Mexico.

"Oh, take me along, will you? I need some Retin-A, and they sell it over-the-counter down there. If I bought it here, I'd have to shell out for a doctor's visit."

"I don't see why not. There's plenty of room...Jeff passed up our invite in favor of a flying lesson."

"Like in an airplane?"

I shuddered. "Yes. Like in an airplane."

There was some push-back from Terry about including Aunt Sally on our trip, and by push-back I mean a great deal of eye-bulging, head-shaking, and a small degree of swearing. In the end, he relented. "But tell her she'll need a passport."

"I'm sure she has one. She went to the Bahamas with Esther a few years ago...though I wouldn't put it past Aunt Sally to have stowed away on the cruise ship."

*****

Friday

With Aunt Sally in the backseat, Terry steered our PT Cruiser south along the I-10 in the predawn darkness. I pulled my purse from beneath the front passenger seat, dumped its contents into my lap, and flipped on the visor light.

"Oh no! It's not here. I think I left it on the kitchen counter."

Terry kept both hands firmly on the wheel and his eyes on the road ahead. "What did you leave on the kitchen counter?"

"My Mexico travel guide."

"We can pick up another one when we get to the border."

"But I wanted to read it on the way."

His sigh was loud enough to make me flinch. "Do you want me to turn around and go back?"

"No, of course not." Actually, I did want him to turn around and go back. I just didn't fancy the idea of *telling* him I wanted him to turn around and go back.

"Why do you even need a guidebook? This isn't a vacation, remember?"

"We have to eat lunch somewhere," I said.

A hand tapped my shoulder, and a ragged-looking paperback was tossed over the seat. "You can look at my travel guide. I can't read it now, anyway…it's too dark. Why did we have to leave at five o'clock in the morning, for Pete's sake?"

I turned in my seat to face Aunt Sally.

"First of all, we left at five o'clock in the morning to beat the rush-hour traffic. Right, Terry?"

"Right." His sidelong glance, in no uncertain terms, said, *I told you so, and I'm never going to let you forget it.*

"Second, this is the official Southern Arizona-Mexican travel guide for 1989–1990."

"I got it for a buck at the library used book sale," said Aunt Sally. "Besides, the really good stuff doesn't change."

I opened to the "Events" section. "Great. Then we can make a stop at Tucson on the way back and make a weekend of it. Sinatra's appearing with Steve Lawrence and Edie Gorme at the Center for the Performing Arts Saturday night."

Terry gave a muffled laugh. "And here I thought I'd missed my last opportunity to see 'Ol' Blue Eyes' on stage."

"I saw Sinatra in Vegas once," said Aunt Sally. "That was in the spring of 1993, back when he was still alive." She leaned forward and jabbed Terry in the back. "Can we stop for breakfast pretty soon? The sun's almost up."

"There's something that looks like a restaurant up ahead on the right," said Terry. "Maybe we could at least get a cup of coffee."

"Or a glass of wine," I muttered under my breath.

My sarcasm went over Aunt Sally's head. "Good idea. It's six a.m., and that's just one letter away from six p.m."

After a quick breakfast, we merged into a growing stream of traffic on the I-10, and conversation turned to what we hoped to find in Mexico.

"Two of the factories are close to each other, about twenty miles south of Nogales," I said. "One is a little farther to the southwest…maybe 15 more miles."

"That's pretty far," Terry said uneasily. "I want to get back on this side of the border before dark."

"That particular factory has its own airstrip," I said, "so we definitely don't want to skip it. Smuggling DDT across the border wouldn't have been much of a challenge."

"We should start with that one then," he suggested.

Terry handed me the map. "Would you take a look and tell me how far we are from the border?"

"You can't be serious." Again, one of the sidebars to my disorder is an inability to filter out trivialities and focus on what's really important. To me, one squiggly line on a map is indistinguishable from another. Terry may as well have asked me to count the stripes on a galloping zebra.

Aunt Sally came to my rescue. "I'll do it," she said, and reached over Terry's shoulder for the map. I watched with envy as she quickly folded it into neat quarters and instantly zeroed in on our route. "Looks like we got 20 miles or so before we reach Nogales."

I took the map from her and stared at it. "I'll take your word for it."

"I hope we can find a drugstore right away," said Aunt Sally. "And I hope we can stop at a Mexican place for lunch."

Terry rolled his eyes. "I don't think that will be a problem."

We'd just parked in a lot on the American side of Nogales, and, passports in hand, were getting ready to join a crowd of pedestrians looking to walk across to the Mexican side, when Aunt Sally said, "It looks like one of our neighbors is headed south of the border, too. Some guy in a black pickup truck has been behind us ever since we gassed up in Sun Lakes."

Chapter Twenty-Three

"That wouldn't be Aaron Hunter, now, would it?" asked Terry.

"If it is, he's not looking all that innocent right now," I said. "Why would he follow us all the way to Mexico?"

"I have an idea," said Aunt Sally. "Maybe we should just ask him."

"I don't think so," I said. "Remember, he matches your description of the guy who broke into Dinah's garage. For all we know, he could be the one who started the landslide that trapped us inside the mine."

Aunt Sally's eyes widened in fear. "So he might be here to try again?!"

Amanda's just speculating now." Terry tugged on my shirtsleeve and pulled me off to the side. "Amanda," he whispered, "You know how your mind works...how you jump to conclusions...you're scaring Aunt Sally."

"I'm scared, too. Our son's best friend was murdered, and most likely Tom. I'm actually trying to do something to help figure this thing out so that we can all move on with our lives. Was I jumping to conclusions when I proposed that those photos we found in Dinah's garage may have been taken on Imfeldt's land? We found the mine and the drums of DDT, didn't we? And Tom's body..."

"Tom's body, *maybe*," Terry reminded me. "You always take your suspicions a step too far. Things are bad enough without you having to exaggerate them. We don't know that the rockslide was rigged any more than we know that the body buried inside that mine is Tom's."

"I wish I were exaggerating," I said, biting my lip to keep my hurt from showing. "Unfortunately, I'm ninety-nine point nine percent sure that I'm not."

"While the two of you were making with the small talk over there, the black truck took off for the opposite end of the lot," said Aunt Sally. "The guy probably parked and is headed this way on foot. Instead of just standing here yapping about it, why don't we get this show on the road?"

We hurried toward the turnstiles that served as the pedestrian doorway to Mexico. A line was beginning to form as more and more people arrived to park in the American lot and walk across the border into Nogales.

"I thought that, by now, Staatz would have at least questioned Hunter about trying to run Dinah and me off the road the other night. That should have been enough incentive for Aaron to stay clear of us."

"Hunter ran you off the road?" asked Aunt Sally, her voice, normally a falsetto, an octave higher than normal.

"Tried to—didn't succeed," I said, ignoring Terry's warning glare.

"And we're only guessing that it might have been him," added Terry. "We don't know for sure that it was."

"Maybe we should call Staatz," I said.

"What can Staatz do from Tempe?" asked Terry. "Have one of the border patrol choppers pick him up and drop him off here in Nogales?"

"Maybe he could call the Nogales Police Department, and they could help us," I suggested.

"Trust me, the Nogales PD already has enough on its plate," said Terry. "Besides, all we have is Aunt Sally's impression that we're being followed."

"It's not an impression," she said, nodding so emphatically that her glasses slid halfway down her nose. "It's a fact."

Terry took my hand as we passed through the turnstile in single file and handed our passports over for inspection. Once on the other side, he said, "The best thing we can do at this point is to try and lose ourselves in the crowd."

"Aunt Sally, I already see four drugstores," I said. "Pick one, and let's get inside and off the street. If Hunter's really out there somewhere, we don't want to give him an easy target."

Aunt Sally chose a pink stucco drugstore whose front entrance featured a tall pillar topped by a gigantic mortar and pestle. "This one looks pretty good. I like pink."

While Aunt Sally made her purchase, Terry and I waited at the front display window, which was covered with hand-lettered signs touting products, most of them generic, claiming to cure every condition or disease imaginable and perhaps a few that hadn't yet been invented. The street outside buzzed with people. Some kept their eyes glued to the path ahead while walking fast and talking on their cell phones, but many seemed to be enjoying a leisurely stroll, stopping frequently to examine outdoor displays of pottery, curios, and clothing. Shop owners held up their wares and happily nodded at the customers' enthusiastic responses to the bargains they were offering. Even in this crowd, Aaron Hunter's significant height would make him hard to miss. I didn't see him, but that didn't mean he wasn't out there somewhere.

Terry spotted a cab parked outside on the street. "Wait here," he said.

Ten minutes later, he returned with a smile on his face. "I just hired Jorge, the cabbie out there, for the day."

"Sounds expensive," I said. "Can't we just drive ourselves? I thought the plan was to go back to the car after lunch and take it through the vehicle crossing back into Mexico."

"It'll be much safer taking a cab. We're going to meet Jorge right here in front of the drugstore at 12:30. I showed him the map, and he says the trip won't take that long...we should be back well before dark."

"Still sounds expensive."

"But well worth it, considering the safety factor. If Hunter is tailing us, he'd have no trouble spotting us in the Cruiser. If we take a cab with Mexican plates, it's unlikely that he'd even notice us, let alone be able to follow us."

Aunt Sally joined us at the window. She smiled as she held up a small shopping bag for our assessment. "I got my Retin-A, and I also found a bottle of my favorite cologne for next to nothing. Esther told me she got some when she was down here a few months ago with her son. I'll bet she got her cologne right here at this very drugstore."

Outside, we joined the growing crowd of shoppers at the open-air market and roamed among stalls of beautifully handmade jewelry and clothing. I chose a sterling silver and turquoise necklace for myself and found an interesting *Dia de los Muertos* leather wrist band, tooled with images of skulls, for Jeff.

Aunt Sally bought a sombrero and immediately perched it on top of her head. "Each of us should buy one of these," she said. "Then we'll blend in with the locals."

"Aunt Sally," said Terry, "the only locals around here are vendors and taxi drivers, and none of them are wearing sombreros."

"We just got here. Trust me, we'll see sombreros."

Though Aunt Sally and I were hoping to have lunch at La Roca, a rustic restaurant built into the side of a cliff and well-known for its colorful ambience and amazing food, Terry thought that if anyone was, indeed, following us, one of the most popular eating spots in Nogales would be the first place he'd look come lunchtime. So we chose Castro's, a small, one-story café that was located a short distance away from the most popular tourist shops and restaurants. Strings of brightly colored lights had been tacked along the dark beam that ran the length of the building and matched the rough-hewn wood doors, which were open so that passersby could enjoy the welcoming strains of mariachi music coming from inside. We walked in to see that a mix of tourists and locals (though Aunt Sally might have argued the point, since none of them were wearing sombreros) were dispersed throughout the restaurant, seated at the bar, or in the roomy booths that lined the walls.

Moving quite smoothly for someone whose bulk would put that of an Arizona Cardinal to shame, the host escorted us to a booth that was centrally located between the front and rear exits. He pointed toward a jovial-looking man working behind the bar and said, "Oscar will be with you in a couple minutes to take your order."

I watched as our host lumbered back to welcome another group, and felt the wooden floor under my feet shake with each footfall. A vague dizziness overcame me, and I hoped it was just hunger and not the onset of a panic attack. I focused on the colorful overlay of ceramic tiles that covered the surface of our table and tried to admire its arrangement of primitive Mexican designs. After a few minutes, I looked up to study the bar, which extended from one end of the room to the other. Along its length, standing between or seated on varnished wooden stools, customers were engaged in lively conversation. Oscar the bartender, a chubby man of about 40, approached our booth. "What can I get for you?"

I unwrapped a paper napkin that had been folded around a set of flatware and used it to dab my face, which was now covered in a cold sweat. I was about to enjoy a wonderful lunch with people whom I loved and trusted, so I was more than a little perturbed that my Cluster C was threatening to spoil the fun. "May I have a wine list, please?"

Someone in the room let out a chortle, but Oscar ignored it and responded to my request. "We don't have a wine list, but I can tell you what we have."

"Okay, what do you have?"

"Red and white."

Another chortle—actually more of a guffaw this time—came from the direction of the bar. Annoyed, Oscar turned to cast a warning look at the offender.

"Perfect," I said. "I'll have white."

"I'll have a Corona," said Terry.

After asking questions about each drink listed on the menu, Aunt Sally finally ordered a margarita. When Oscar returned with the drinks, I asked him where the ladies room was.

He nodded toward an archway at the back of the restaurant. "Right through that doorway."

"Are you okay?" asked Terry.

"Feeling a bit woozy, is all. I just need to splash some cold water on my face. I'll be right back."

By the time I'd reached the archway, the room had started to spin. The door to the ladies room was locked, but I saw an exit sign on the far wall. I raced to the door, pulled it open, and used my purse to jam it so it wouldn't close and lock me out. I stepped outside into the rear parking lot and inhaled a little bit of air and a whole lot of dust. A black cat meandered across my path, arched his back, and hissed at my unwelcome appearance before padding off toward a huge trash bin that was overflowing with garbage.

I leaned against the building and closed my eyes against the noonday sun. A hot wind was blowing, and sandy dirt from an empty tract of land next to the parking lot was whirling through the air in staccato bursts, making it thick and yellow. I tried to breathe normally, without hyperventilating or swallowing too much grit. When I opened my eyes, the first thing I saw was a black pickup truck parked just inside the entrance to the parking lot. There was no mistaking the man behind the wheel: It was Aaron Hunter.

Chapter Twenty-Four

The door to the parking lot swung open with a creak. "Amanda? Are you all right? What are you doing out here?" Terry picked up my handbag. "What's your purse doing on the floor?"

I grabbed my handbag with one hand and pushed him back inside with the other. "Quick...get inside. Aaron Hunter's here."

Terry pushed the door open wider and held a hand over his mouth to deflect the gusting clouds of sand. "Where?"

I pointed to the parking place closest to the lot entrance. "There." I was pointing at an empty space. "But he was there just a second ago."

Terry reached for my hand. "Come on. Let's get lunch over and done with so we can leave."

We shared family-sized platters of burritos, tacos, and something I'd never before tasted, which turned out to be my favorite: *pollo encacahuatado*, a traditional chicken dish that was heavily flavored with garlic and peanut sauce. Despite the fact that Terry, thinking it would make her more jittery than she already was, warned me not to, I told Aunt Sally about spotting Aaron Hunter in the parking lot.

"So why doesn't Staatz just arrest the guy?" she asked.

"Because there's no proof that he's done anything wrong," I said. "At this point, it's just a theory."

"Your theory," added Terry. "Let's suppose, for a minute, that he's innocent. We still have to consider

Dieter Imfeldt. He had both motive and opportunity to get rid of Tom."

"And there's also Steven Bryce," I said. "He had motive, and more than enough time to follow Aunt Sally and me to the mine and then come back for that Caterpillar."

Aunt Sally folded her arms in front of her and shook her head. "I still don't see how either of those guys could be connected to poor Nathan's murder."

"They may not be connected at all…it might just be a horrible coincidence," said Terry. "Remember what Staatz said. There's still a chance that Nathan's murder may have been a random act…the result of an armed robbery gone bad."

"Maybe Aunt Sally's right," I said. "Maybe it *is* time to have a face-to-face with Hunter."

"It may not be the worst thing in the world. In my opinion, if he wanted to make trouble for us on this trip, he'd have done it by now. But here's the question of the day…if he's so innocent, then why is he following us?"

Aunt Sally and I waited inside the restaurant while Terry scoped out the area. Minutes later, he opened the door and motioned for us to join him. "All clear."

We walked fast, keeping away from the street, preferring to stay close to the buildings and to lose ourselves in the lunchtime crowds milling along the sidewalks. I was relieved to see that Jorge, a jovial man sporting a trim moustache, khaki shirt, and baggy jeans, was waiting for us next to his cab, which was parked in front of the pharmacy.

With a final glance over his shoulder to survey the crowds for any sign of Aaron Hunter or his truck, Terry nodded for us to get into the taxi. While he climbed into the front passenger seat, Jorge ushered me and Aunt Sally into the back. We were happy to discover that he was fluent in English, and he enthusiastically agreed to serve as our translator for the trip.

Our first planned stop, the farthest from the border and about twenty miles south of Nogales, was Matesa Industriales, located southeast of the Parque Industrial Nuevo Nogales, near the town of Cibuta. Jorge quickly maneuvered his way through the winding streets of Nogales to the outskirts of the city. Men, both young and old, huddled in animated conversations on street corners and at entrances to stores. Women pushed strollers along paths composed of dirt and chunks of concrete, sidewalks that had seen better days and were now in need of repair or repaving. A group of teen-aged girls wearing short skirts and high-heeled boots sauntered along the side of the street and glanced with disinterest at our passing vehicle. It was apparent that we'd left behind the tourist area—and hopefully, Aaron Hunter.

We drove along Highway 15, leaving the city limits of Nogales and entering the rural areas of Sonora, which greatly resembled the Arizona terrain with the exception of the roads.

"The conditions down here are pretty rough," said Terry. "I don't think the PT Cruiser would have even been up to the trip."

Jorge shrugged. "If the roads haven't crumbled away to nothing out here, we consider them to be good."

"I'll tell you another thing that's good down here: the drugstores." Aunt Sally pulled her bottle of cologne from the shopping bag, unscrewed the cap, and leaned forward to hold it up to Jorge's nose. "I can't even afford to buy 'White Shoulders' at the discount mall anymore. Go ahead and take a sniff, Jorge."

When Jorge lowered his head to smell the cologne, his gaze left the path ahead just long enough to avoid seeing a large pothole. The cab bounced so violently that for a few seconds, the force of it lifted us from our seats. Aunt Sally shrieked as the bottle left her grip and fell into Jorge's lap. A horrible, acrid odor immediately filled the cab's interior. Uttering a stream of angry Spanish words that made me glad I'd taken French in high school, Jorge pulled the cab to the side of the road and jumped out. His jeans, from the crotch to just above the knees, were soaked. "Dios maldito!"

"Sorry, Jorge," said Aunt Sally, "but no *habla español.*"

Terry picked up the bottle. "No offense, Aunt Sally, but this cologne smells like old shoes that have been soaked in formaldehyde."

"It does, now that you mention it," said Aunt Sally, taking the bottle from Terry. "But look. It says 'Hombres Bronco,' just like Esther's bottle: That's Spanish for 'White Shoulders.'"

I unrolled my window all the way and said, "I don't think so, Aunt Sally. I'm pretty sure that 'blanco' is the Spanish word for 'white.'"

All the windows were now wide open, but the stench of the cologne was still wreaking havoc on our ability to breathe and causing our eyes to water profusely.

"Here," I said, handing out wads of tissue. "Use these to cover your nose and mouth."

Terry took the bottle from Aunt Sally and joined Jorge outside on the side of the road. Dust devils were swirling in profusion around the cab, but, at least for Jorge and Terry, a mouthful of sand was apparently preferable to further exposure to the maleficent odor of Aunt Sally's cologne. "Jorge, does this label say 'White Shoulders?'"

Jorge held the bottle up close to his face, and immediately jerked it away in disgust. "No, Senor. This is the cheapest men's cologne in all of Mexico. Your aunt meant to purchase 'Hombros Blanco,' but this is

'Hombres Broncos'—in English, you would say 'Rough Men.'" His initial anger quickly gave way to the humor of the situation. He flashed a white smile, then quickly closed his mouth against the blowing dust. He replaced the tissue he'd been holding with a large handkerchief that he pulled from his pocket and held it to his face as he spoke. "Farmers around here use it to keep the horseflies away."

Despite the fact that we had to keep our faces covered, we all burst into fits of laughter. Even Aunt Sally's doleful expression eventually turned to a grin. There was a positive side to the cologne fiasco: The episode had completely erased any tension we were feeling about being followed by a possible murderer. We waited another 15 minutes for the stench in the taxi's interior to dissipate. By the time we got underway, the foulness of the air inside the cab had been reduced to a tolerable level. Unfortunately, the seats and floor quickly had become covered with the sand that had blown in through the open windows and doors.

"I'll add an extra 25 dollars to the fee we agreed on, Jorge," said Terry. "That should cover a good cleaning. If you take her into the carwash, maybe they'll be able to do something about the smell."

In our hurry to escape the lingering odor of "Hombres Broncos," we fairly erupted from the cab when Jorge pulled into the parking space at Matesa Industriales. Tall smokestacks that sent black plumes of smoke into the air, several huge vats, and piles of sulfur resembling ancient sand dunes merged to lend a decidedly ominous tone to the factory's surroundings. We made our way through double glass doors into a brightly lit reception area that could have been found in any American factory. The receptionist, a petite woman in her mid-fifties with a pleasant smile and a taut

French twist, greeted us as we entered. The nameplate on her desk said Anita Reyes. Her smile dissolved as she crinkled her nose at the fumes emanating from Jorge's clothing.

"Sorry," I said. "We had a little accident with some cologne in the car, and Jorge got the worst of it."

Jorge elucidated in Spanish, and Anita nodded in sympathy before turning to address us as a group. "How may I help you?"

While Aunt Sally and Terry took seats in comfortable-looking occasional chairs facing the reception desk, I stepped forward and pulled a manila folder containing Tom's photos from my purse. "We need to talk to someone who was with Matesa ten years ago. We have some pictures we'd like to ask them about."

The woman folded her arms in a guarded stance. "What kind of pictures?"

I handed the photos, one by one, to Anita. "The drums in these photos were found in an abandoned copper mine near Jerome, Arizona. We just need to have someone take a look at them and tell us if they originated from this factory."

Anita glanced briefly at the photos, and quickly handed them back to me. "No. These do not belong to Matesa."

"Are you sure?" I asked, and offered the photos to her again. "We've come a long way. Do you mind taking one more look?"

She made a show of examining the pictures, but there was no mistaking the perfunctory nature of her effort. She shook her head emphatically. "No. They are not from Matesa."

"Do you know that for sure?" I asked.

Anita tossed me a look of annoyance and nodded. "I was here ten years ago. I would know if they were our containers."

"Jorge," I said, turning to our cabbie/interpreter. "Maybe Spanish would clarify things a bit. Can you please try to make Anita understand how important this is to us? Ask her again if she's certain that the drums in the photos didn't come from this factory. And if not, does she have any idea where they might have come from?"

While Jorge engaged Anita in a conversation that seemed inordinately long and which, despite her proximity to Jorge and his cologne-saturated clothing, brought more than one smile to her face, I moved to a wall that was covered with photos depicting Matesa's history. A framed collage of older photos featuring the original factory showed it to be a much smaller operation, but no less ominous-looking, than the current one. Pictures of the groundbreaking for the new factory, on which the date June 10, 1995, was printed, portrayed the smiling owner, Ramon Matesa, cutting a ribbon with an oversized pair of scissors. Other photos contained scenes of happy workers diligently manning various assembly lines and loading their products into semi-trailers for transport. There were also pictures of Matesa and his wife boarding the corporate jet at the company's airstrip, which, according to what Terry and I had seen on Google Earth, was located well behind the property's main building and about five miles off the highway. Three smaller planes were lined up in the far left background.

Jorge smiled his thanks to Anita, who, without bidding us adios, went back to her desk and immediately became engrossed in whatever was on her computer screen. On the way to the car, he shrugged his apology. "I'm sorry, Senora. I tried, but I'm afraid that Miss Anita was not very helpful."

In the taxi, he started the engine and asked, "What is our next stop?"

"We can head back to Nogales," I said as I quickly unrolled my side window.

"Nogales?" said Terry. "What about the other two factories?"

"We don't have to look further to find out where those drums originated. They came from Matesa."

"But…"

"I'll explain later," I said.

"Can we make one more stop at the drugstore?" asked Aunt Sally, her voice pleading. "I'll get the right stuff this time. And I promise not to take it out of the bag."

As we drove north toward the border, Terry and Jorge engaged in good-natured arguing about which was better, American football or Mexican soccer (to Jorge's consternation, Terry refused to call it football), while Aunt Sally gazed dreamily at the passing scenery.

I took the photograph I'd copped from the wall in Matesa's reception office from my purse and offered it to Terry. "I'm adding this photo to the ones we hand over to Detective Staatz. I think he's going to find it very interesting."

Chapter Twenty-Five

Jorge was all smiles when he dropped us off at the drugstore, and I'm not sure if it was because he was happy to see us heading back to our side of the border, or if he was exceedingly anxious to get home and shower off the remains of "Hombres Broncos." I suspect it was a little of both. Terry and I waited outside while Aunt Sally made her purchase.

"I got the right stuff this time," she said as she emerged from the store. "But I got another bottle of 'Hombres Broncos' for Esther. She's got scorpions, and this should do the trick. If it works for horseflies, it's gotta work for scorpions, right?"

The wind had lulled to a mild breeze, and the air was warm and clear as dusk fell. We made our way to the pedestrian turnstiles, stopping only to purchase some fish tacos from a street vendor. Feeling a bit giddy about being on U.S. soil again, we chatted and enjoyed a laugh-filled rehash of Aunt Sally's cologne mishap as we walked to the parking lot. Our collective happy mood evaporated when we saw Aaron Hunter, his arms folded, leaning against the Cruiser.

"Well, we said we should think about a face-to-face with Hunter," I said. "It looks like we're about to get our wish."

Hunter lifted a hand in a languid wave when he saw us. His familiar black pickup was parked in the space next to the Cruiser.

"Something wrong, Hunter?" asked Terry. "Need a jump?"

"Everything's fine, Mr. Winters. But I think you folks may have gotten the wrong idea about me. I thought it was time we had a talk."

"It's been a long day, Aaron," I said. "Maybe our conversation should wait until Detective Staatz is able to join us. I know he'll probably have some questions for you. Like why you broke into Dinah's garage…and why you tried to run Dinah and me off the road the other night."

Aaron closed his eyes and shook his head in a show of disbelief. For the second time, the thought that he could be in show business crossed my mind. Not only did he have a singer's voice…he could act, too.

"That wasn't me."

Aunt Sally thrust her drugstore bag at him. "Don't play innocent, Hunter. Why have you been stalking us all the way across the border, you dirty, rotten no good son of a b—"

"Lady, who *are* you?" asked Aaron, his face turning red. He moved away from the Cruiser and dropped his arms to his side, his fists clenched. His frame was imposing, and not a little intimidating, and for every step he took toward us, we took two steps backward. "I've seen you before."

"This is my Aunt Sally," I said as I wrapped a protective arm around her slight shoulders. Despite her show of bravado, she was shaking.

Terry moved to stand between Hunter and the rest of us. "Why have you been following us?"

"Because my father asked me to. He's afraid something bad might happen."

Aunt Sally took off her glasses, wiped the lenses with a handkerchief, and said, "Turn around, Hunter."

"What?"

"You heard me." She held out a hand and rotated it slowly. "I said, 'turn around.'"

Hunter questioned me with a look, and I pleaded innocence with a shrug.

He obediently turned around to face the Cruiser so that his back was facing us.

"Nope, it's not him," said Aunt Sally. "He's too tall."

"Are you sure?" I asked as I studied Hunter, my gaze moving up and down his frame.

"What are you talking about?" asked Hunter, turning to face us once again.

"Aunt Sally's description of the man who broke into Mrs. Reynold's garage the day of Nathan's funeral made us think that maybe it was you," said Terry.

Hunter snickered. "Wow, you people must think I'm the scum of the earth."

"Count yourself lucky," said Aunt Sally, pointing to her bag. "I'm armed and dangerous. If I thought you were the hippie thief that pushed Amanda and me into those bushes, you'd be stinking to high heaven right now."

Aaron shook his head in bewilderment. "I have no idea what that even means."

"You said that it wasn't you who tried to run Dinah and me off the road," I said. "You're lying...I distinctly remember seeing your truck behind us."

"You're right about one thing...I followed you that night. And I admit that I've been watching Mrs. Reynolds' house...like I said, my father asked me to keep an eye on things. I saw the two of you take off in the Audi, and I was behind you all the way to Alma School. But another truck showed up and was tailing me. Then all of a sudden, he cut around in front of me. He's the one who tried to push you through the red light—not me. I tried to catch up to him, but he got away from me."

"I don't remember seeing a second truck that night," I said.

"I don't know, Amanda," suggested Terry. "In the confusion, you could have easily missed it."

Aaron fixed his gaze on me. "I know what happened to you and—" He glanced nervously at Aunt Sally. "—your aunt, here, in the mine. I was there."

"You're the one who called 9-1-1?" asked Terry.

"But I thought *I* called 9-1-1," I said, frowning in confusion.

"That explains it," said Aunt Sally. "When I checked my phone, I noticed that '9-1-1' wasn't in the call history. I figured it must have been a glitch."

"I was in my truck at the edge of the foothills," said Aaron. "After the rock slide, I looked up and got a glimpse of yellow through the trees."

"The Caterpillar we saw in Imfeldt's garage," I said.

"By the time I got to the clearing just above the entrance to the mine, whoever had been there was already gone."

Terry was fuming. "Why did you wait so long before calling it in? They were inside that mine for hours!"

"I tried to clear away some of the rock at the entrance and dropped my phone. It landed in a crevice, and it took me nearly an hour to get it out. It sounds stupid, I know. But it's the truth. Once I found my phone, I called it in right away."

"Then we have you to thank for saving our lives," I said numbly.

"Like I said, my father believes there might be more trouble before Nathan's killer is done."

"By more trouble, do you mean more murders?" I asked.

He answered with a nod.

"If you or your father knows who killed Nathan, you need to go to Detective Staatz," said Terry. "And you have to tell him what you saw at the mine."

Hunter shook his head. "We first thought that it might have been Imfeldt who killed Nathan. But now, it's obvious we were wrong. Dead men don't drive Caterpillars."

"What about Steven Bryce?" I suggested. "He used to work with Nathan's father. He was furious after Imfeldt's account was taken away from him and given to Tom. We ran into Bryce at Imfeldt's estate just before we got trapped in the mine. He's Imfeldt's attorney—at least, he was..."

"I asked my father about Bryce," said Aaron, "but he said he never met the guy. He doesn't think Bryce has anything to do with this."

I told Hunter about the discoveries of the grave and Tom's Triumph. What I didn't tell him about was finding Tom's photos in Dinah's garage and our real reason for traveling to Nogales. We'd managed to shake him off our trail by taking the cab to Matesa Industriales. If Hunter's acting skills were the reason I was beginning to believe him, I wanted to keep that final ace tucked up my sleeve.

Aaron asked about our trip to Mexico, and I took the lead by telling him that it was a shopping excursion. I was particularly relieved when Aunt Sally took the clue and went along with my story. I wasn't thoroughly convinced that Aaron was telling the whole truth, but I had to admit that his story made as much sense as anything else. Tom's photos, along with the one I'd snatched from under Anita's nose in the Matesa Industriales office, could be the key to unraveling this whole thing. The sooner we delivered that evidence to Staatz, the better.

Hunter followed us all the way back to Sun Lakes. After dropping off Aunt Sally, Terry and I arrived home to find the TV running at full volume and the living room taken over by Jeff and his friends. Several pizza boxes, most of them empty except for a few remnants of crust, covered the coffee table and a large part of the floor. Completing the tableau were bottles of Corona Extra, with wedges of lime floating in the amber liquid, scattered here and there among the pizza boxes.

Jeff jumped up from the sofa. "Mom! Dad! I thought you were going to Mexico."

"We did go to Mexico," I said. "We're back now."

I recognized Danielle Palmer, and the remaining five students looked vaguely familiar…attendees at Nathan's funeral, I thought.

Everyone got to their feet and stood awkwardly, offering Terry and me little waves or nods of greeting.

Terry's gazed scanned the group. "Uh, I trust that everyone here is at least 21?"

Seven heads nodded enthusiastically.

Jeff said, "We were watching *Iron Man* in honor of Nate. It's—it was his favorite movie."

"And pizza was his favorite food," added Danielle. "Tonight is the two-week anniversary of his death, and we wanted to do something, you know, in his honor."

"Seeing as it's a Friday night and Dad doesn't have to get up for work in the morning, you all go ahead and finish the movie," I said.

"That's okay. We were just watching the bonus stuff," said Jeff. "We finished the movie an hour ago." He turned to his guests and added, "Maybe we should call it a night, guys. I have to be at the airport early tomorrow morning for a flying lesson, anyway."

"Another one?" I groaned. "But you just had one today."

"Mr. Palmer had to cancel today to go to some emergency staff meeting."

"And here I was so happy that the flying lesson was behind us."

"Don't worry, Mrs. Winters," said Danielle. "My dad flies out of Phoenix-Mesa Gateway. It has a really good safety record...the last accident there was in 2010, and nobody even died."

I was about to respond to that, but Terry pushed me gently toward the master bedroom. We were so exhausted that we didn't bother to turn on the TV. There was no way my brain, however, was going to let me sleep. It was on overdrive, buzzing with "what-ifs." *What if* the body in the grave turned out not to be Tom, after all? *What if* Nathan had been murdered, as Dinah once said, "all because of a lousy bike"? *What if* Dieter Imfeldt really did commit suicide out of depression over his declining health? Even if all those what-ifs were true, I told myself, they didn't explain what happened at the mine, or why Tom's Triumph had been sitting in Dieter Imfeldt's garage for the past decade. I supposed that if Tom wanted to start a new life, he would have sold the car, and Imfeldt, a well-known car collector, would have been an eager buyer. But what about the Disney tickets Tom had shown to Anthony Hunter? The what-ifs didn't explain those either unless Hunter had lied about them. All we had was Aaron and Anthony Hunter's word that they were both telling the truth.

A thought occurred to me, and I sat up in bed and turned on my lamp. "Terry, do you have access to news footage of the tribal protests from ten years ago?"

"We keep everything for, like, forever," he said sleepily. "I might be able to find something in our old video files. What are you looking for?"

"I'm not sure. I'd be interested to see what's on that footage, though."

"I'll check out the station archives tomorrow."

I punched my pillow into a comfortable shape and, from the corner of my eye, saw the red message light blinking on the answering machine on Terry's nightstand. "Uh-oh," I said. "There's a message."

Terry played it back on speaker mode. It was Staatz calling to let us know that the DNA results came back early on the remains found in the mine. "Sergeant Farwell called in a favor, and the Prescott folks were happy to oblige. The remains found in that grave do belong to Tom Reynolds. And it was definitely murder. Looks like someone took a rock to his skull. Anyway, I wanted to give you a heads-up. I caught Mrs. Reynolds just as she was getting ready to leave for Tucson. I'm going over to give her the news tomorrow morning, and I'd like for you to be there."

Chapter Twenty-Six
Saturday

I awoke at five a.m. to the sound of a demonic voice echoing through the house: "YOU'RE BA-A-A-D, PLE-E-ASE GO-O-O! YOU'RE BA-A-A-D, PLE-E-ASE GO-O-O!"

My first reaction was to bury my head under the covers and scoot across the width of our king-size bed to cling to Terry for protection. Unbelievably, the man continued to snore softly into his pillow like a puppy cuddled up to its mother. The horrible voice continued its chilling threat, over and over: "YOU'RE BA-A-A-D, PLE-E-ASE GO-O-O!" It was so loud that my ears were ringing.

I poked Terry in the back, and when that didn't work, grabbed hold of an arm and shook it. "Terry, wake up!"

"Huh?!" His eyes fluttering, he rolled over and looked at me as if I was the one from whom the voice from hell was emanating.

"What is that?!" I asked, wondering if some of Jerome's ghosts had followed us home and had decided that they wanted the house to themselves.

"YOU'RE BA-A-A-D, PLE-E-ASE GO-O-O!" The ghost may have been loud, but at least it was polite.

I covered my ears. "Make it stop!"

Terry jumped up out of bed, and Jeff appeared in the doorway. "Mom! Dad! What's that ungodly racket?!"

Huddled together like the Scooby gang, we made our way to the kitchen, the room that seemed to be the source of the hair-raising threat.

Terry stared up at a corner of the ceiling. "Well, I'll be. It's the smoke alarm."

We stood and listened as the small plastic disc screamed at us to "PLE-E-EASE GO-O-O!" Then Terry started to laugh. "It's not saying, 'You're bad, please go.' It's saying, 'Your ba—a—tterey's—low.'"

"Oh…our battery's low," said Jeff.

"Uh-huh. I get it," I said. "There are about four others in the house that look just like this one. Why on earth would Dad have installed smoke alarms that sound like Mercedes McCambridge's voice in *The Exorcist*?"

"I don't know," said Terry, as he jabbed a mop handle at the alarm to silence it. "But first thing tomorrow I'll check them all out and replace them with the normal, non-scary ones that just chirp."

"Jeez-Louise," said Jeff. "No wonder Grandpa had a heart attack."

None of us could even think of going back to bed, so I made a wake-up breakfast of strong coffee, pancakes, and sausage. Terry set the table and cut up a cantaloupe while Jeff showered.

At the kitchen table, I passed Jeff the syrup and said, "Maybe you should hold off on that flying lesson today. You don't want to be behind the controls of an airplane after getting less than a full night's sleep."

Jeff rolled his eyes. "Mom, I'll be fine. I would have gotten up early, anyway. Besides, it's not like Mr. Palmer's going to let me fly solo today or anything. It's only my first lesson…I'll probably just sit in the cockpit and watch him at the controls."

I gave Jeff the kind of hug normally reserved for a soldier going off to war. When he was finally able to unlock my arms from around his neck, he said, "Don't worry, Mom. It'll be fine."

"I hate airplanes," I said to Terry as he drove me to Dinah's. "Especially those little ones. You always hear about them on the nightly news. They crash into mountains or fall on top of houses and kill people in their beds while they're watching *The Tonight Show*."

Terry assured me that Jeff was in safe hands. "I'm sure Marty Palmer is a seasoned pilot."

I paused with my hand on the door handle before getting out of the car. "Do we know that for sure? I mean, do we know anything about him, really?"

"He teaches aeronautics at ASU."

"Aeronautic management technology," I corrected.

"You'd better get going. Staatz is pulling up behind us."

"Will you call me if you find something interesting on that protest footage?"

"You know I will." He leaned over and kissed me goodbye. "Now go…and good luck with Dinah."

Staatz greeted me with a nod. "I appreciate your being here, Mrs. Winters."

"How much does Dinah know?" I asked. "What did you tell her?"

"I told her about your finding the DDT in Imfeldt's mine, but I didn't mention the grave. All I said was that I had an update on Tom and that I wanted both of you to hear it."

We were halfway up the path when Dinah opened the door. "Good morning."

"Morning," Staatz and I said in unison.

I noticed that Staatz was unable to keep his eyes off Dinah. I couldn't fault him for it. Dressed in a white peasant blouse and a black skirt decorated with teal bric-a-brac, she looked particularly gorgeous that morning. Silver hoop earrings were her only jewelry. With her dark, wavy hair and smoky eyes, she could have been a Romany princess. I thought that it might be a crime to look that good before nine a.m.

There was no coffee this time. Dinah sat numbly on the corner of the sectional, and Staatz and I took separate chairs facing her.

Staatz cleared his throat and said with a professional stiffness that convinced me he'd rehearsed what he was about to say, "Mrs. Reynolds, I'm sorry to inform you that the DNA evidence confirmed that the remains found in Imfeldt's mine are those of your husband. He was murdered."

"How?"

Staatz stared down at the floor. "Do you really want to know?"

"Yes, I do."

"According to the medical examiner, it was blunt-force trauma. A rock, most likely."

A sound came out of Dinah's mouth that she'd intended to be a word but passed between her lips in a low groan. I moved over to her and placed my arms around her as if she were my child. She wept, and I held her tightly, her head buried in my neck, until there were no tears left. Staatz waited a few more minutes before he continued.

"Like I said, the drums in that mine did contain DDT. It looks like Imfeldt got nervous at some point and decided to hide evidence that could incriminate him at the hearings. He believed no one would think to look there, right on his own land...and when the charges against him were dropped, he figured that no one would ever have reason to search his property."

I studied Dinah's face intently. I'd been expecting another emotional collapse. I think Staatz had been too, or he wouldn't have asked me to be present. But there was no collapse. There was only numbness...inordinate calmness. I would have preferred some form of hysterics from her. I remembered how calm she'd appeared at the jail, just before she'd swallowed those pills.

The shadow of a cheerless smile broke through the mask to add a trace of animation to her face. She glanced toward me, then back to Staatz. "I imagine that you still don't know who killed Tom any more than you know who murdered Nate."

"No, I don't. Not yet."

"Dinah," I said, "if it's okay with you, I'll be giving Tom's photos to Detective Staatz."

"Of course. I'm just going to get some water. Would either of you like some?"

"No thanks," I said.

Staatz' voice was almost apologetic. "I'm good."

Dinah moved past us on her way to the kitchen, her skirt swishing the air just enough to leave the light musk scent of Ralph Loren's "Notorious" in her wake.

Again, Staatz watched her until she disappeared into the hallway. There was something there, all right. There was no mistaking the look in his eyes. I took the opportunity to tell him about our trip to Mexico and the visit to Matesa Industriales.

"The drums in those mines came from that factory," I said. "The ones in a photo I found in the office match the ones in Tom's pictures. The picture's there with the others."

Before accepting the manila envelope from me, he smoothed his hair with both hands, a gesture which I now recognized as a nervous habit, not unlike my teeth-grinding. "Mrs. Winters, I've got to tell you that you have this annoying habit of talking around whatever point it is you're trying to make."

I cleared my throat. "The point, Detective, is that we now know that Aaron Hunter and his father are both innocent. Aaron followed us to Nogales, and..."

"He followed you?"

"His father asked him to look out for us." I pursed my lips and continued, "Anthony believes that the murderer isn't finished yet. I've come to the conclusion that Dieter Imfeldt, or someone who worked for him, killed both Tom and Nathan."

Dinah came back into the room in time to catch my last formulation. "Detective Staatz, do you think Steven Bryce could be involved?"

"For the past ten years, Bryce has been Imfeldt's personal attorney," I added. "I sort of ran into him at Imfeldt's estate the day Aunt Sally and I got trapped in the mine."

"Even if I buy your suggestion that Bryce had a motive to kill Tom," said Staatz, "what would his motive be for killing Nathan?"

I wish I'd brought the notes I'd been working on for weeks. I forged ahead from memory and tried to keep my voice calm and rational. "He wanted to suppress evidence that he mistakenly believed Nathan had discovered—Tom's photos of those drums of DDT being loaded into the mine on Imfeldt's property. If Nathan connected with Imfeldt by phone to arrange a meeting with him, it would have been logical for Imfeldt to consult his attorney, Bryce. I mean, Imfeldt was old, but he knew that those drums of DDT were still in the mine, and he also knew that Tom was buried there. Maybe Imfeldt talked to Bryce about his options…maybe even told him that he wanted to confess before it was too late."

Dinah said, "Bryce could have killed Nate, and then Imfeldt, to stop him from going to the police, if for no other reason than to preserve the hefty retainer I imagine Imfeldt was paying him."

"Did they find anything on those soil samples from the Caterpillar in Imfeldt's garage?" I asked Staatz. "Did they match the dirt outside the mine?"

He shook his head. "The tests were inconclusive. The samples could have come from anywhere within miles of Imfeldt's estate." He opened the manila envelope and drew the photos from it.

When he saw Dinah and me exchange frustrated glances, he said, "This isn't *CSI: Miami*, you know. In real life, evidence doesn't come tied up so nice and neat like a birthday present."

"That photo on top is the one from Matesa Industriales," I said.

He removed his glasses and rubbed his eyes. "Which I'm assuming you stole."

"Borrowed," I said. "I have every intention of returning it just as soon as you wrap up this case…which, now that you have this evidence, I trust will be soon."

He slid the photos back into the envelope and stood. "Mrs. Winters, once again, I need to warn you to leave the investigation to me." He glanced at Dinah before focusing on me with a look that made my stomach churn. "If you continue to interfere with this investigation or withhold evidence, I'll have no choice but to charge you with obstruction of justice."

"Tell me something," I said. "Would *your* investigation have taken you to the abandoned copper mine on Imfeldt's property? Or to Mexico, and Matesa Industriales?"

He chose not to answer and said, "I'll see myself out. Mrs. Reynolds, do you still have my card?"

"I have it. Thank you, Detective. But I'll be leaving for Tucson tomorrow morning."

"Regardless, feel free to call me any time, day or night."

I noticed that he didn't extend the same offer to me.

Shortly after we'd left for Sun Lakes, Dinah's cell phone rang. "It's Terry," she said, and handed me the phone.

"Did you find something on that footage?" I asked.

"I sure did. Is Staatz still there?"

"No, he just left. Dinah's driving me home right now."

"Well, you'd both better come down to the station and have a look at this video for yourselves. And while you're at it, you may want to call Staatz and have him join us."

I tossed Dinah a conspiratorial look. "Uh, let's hold off on that...we can get him involved if we need to. But what is it? What did you find?"

"It's not 'what' I found that's so interesting...it's 'who.'"

Chapter Twenty-Seven

Dinah and I walked into the TV station to find Terry waiting for us in the front lobby. I started to ask him questions at the reception desk, but he shushed me with a brief kiss. "Not here."

After obtaining visitor badges from the receptionist and leading us through a maze of narrow hallways to a tiny viewing room at the back of the building, he motioned for Dinah and me to take seats at a long conference table and picked up a remote control. A moment later, a screen on the wall in front of us flashed to life.

"Okay, I've got the footage cued up," said Terry, nodding at the screen. "Watch."

"What's that building?" I asked.

"Ten years ago, it was Imfeldt's corporate headquarters. He moved the main office to his estate about three years ago when his health started to go downhill. Right now, you're looking at the south end of his cotton fields. In the upper right-hand corner, you can just make out the beginning of an airstrip."

The camera zoomed in on the protesters in front of the main building. We watched, entranced, as what looked to be about one hundred Pima tribal officials, men, women, and children carrying signs (JUSTICE FOR OUR MOTHERS AND CHILDREN!! PROTECT OUR LAND, RIVERS, AND STREAMS—ARREST DIETER IMFELDT!), marched back and forth while chanting in their native tongue.

"I wonder what they're saying," I said.

"Most likely, they're praying for Imfeldt's downfall…or worse."

"It obviously didn't work," Dinah said. "I read that at the time of his death, he was one of the wealthiest men in the Valley."

Terry shook his head. "And no one was ever able to prove that he'd been using DDT on his crops—not until, that is, Amanda found those drums in the mine on his property. And get this…the cotton fields Imfeldt farmed back then didn't actually belong to him. He leased the land from the Gila River Indian Reservation."

"So as far as the Pimas were concerned, Imfeldt was a murderer, and he was using their own tainted land and water supply as his murder weapon," said Dinah. "I can almost understand why Anthony Hunter sent those emails to Tom."

"Couldn't the Pimas just take their land back?" I asked. "Kick Imfeldt to the curb?"

"There was a long-term contract…so no," said Terry. "Okay…the part I want you to see is coming up. Watch. Look who's standing just outside the front entrance to the building."

I expected to see Steven Bryce, but I was wrong. "Wait a minute—freeze it right there," I said. I stood and moved closer to the screen. I turned to Terry and Dinah. "Is that Marty Palmer?!"

Dinah joined me in front of the screen. "If it isn't, he has a twin."

As something caught my eye on the airstrip in the background, my stomach performed a maneuver that was a combination barrel roll, spin, and loop. "And that plane is exactly like one in the photo from Matesa Industriales."

*****

In the Audi on the way home from the station, I borrowed Dinah's phone to call Jeff. The call went directly to voice mail.

"What time was his flying lesson?" Dinah asked as she pulled into Sun Lakes.

"I don't know! Why doesn't he answer?!" I tried his number five more times, but continued to get his voice mail.

I called Detective Staatz next, and to my surprise, he picked up right away.

"Mrs. Winters. How can I help you? Or are you calling to tell me about some more evidence you've been holding out on me?"

"Actually, I'm calling about some new evidence that's just now come to light…"

"What is it this time?"

I put him on speaker phone for Dinah's benefit. "Marty Palmer, the father of Nathan's girlfriend, Danielle, was connected somehow to Dieter Imfeldt ten years ago. Terry found some old news footage of the Pima protests, and Dinah and I just watched it. Palmer was standing right there in front of Imfeldt's headquarters, plain as day."

"I'm sorry, Mrs. Winters, but that's not exactly evidence, and it's definitely not new."

"What do you mean?"

"I mean that I already knew Marty Palmer had worked for Imfeldt. He was Imfeldt's corporate pilot back then. In fact, he was the pilot who sprayed Imfeldt's cotton fields."

"Marty Palmer is a crop duster?!"

"Was. He left Imfeldt's employment shortly after the hearings and finished up his teaching degree. He's been with ASU for the last seven years."

"Jeff might be in a plane with Palmer at this very moment," I said, my voice shaking.

"Mrs. Winters, all that news footage proves is that Palmer used to work for Dieter Imfeldt. There's no reason to believe he's involved in anything related to the Reynolds' murders."

"I had bad feelings about Palmer from the start," I said, staring into the phone as though I were staring into Staatz's eyes.

Dinah gave me a side glance. "That's what you said about Aaron Hunter. Remember?"

Staatz cleared his throat. "Mrs. Winters, I'm only telling you this because I know you're worried about your son's association with Palmer. I'm pretty close to making an arrest in Tom's case."

"You are?! Who?!"

"Steven Bryce. Bryce had both motive and opportunity, and the Scottsdale PD found some pretty damning evidence among Imfeldt's personal papers. Bryce offered to get rid of Tom, along with the evidence he was going to bring to the hearings, in exchange for a position as Imfeldt's attorney. Imfeldt accepted his offer. I also believe that Bryce may have 'arranged' Richard May's car accident, though I doubt that I'll be able to prove it. Tom's case notes indicate that May had been willing to join him in testifying against Imfeldt at the hearings."

"What about Nathan?" asked Dinah, her voice barely audible. "Did Bryce kill him, too?"

"I don't have a case there, yet, but I'm confident that I will very soon. It looks like Imfeldt mentioned to Bryce that he was going to meet with Nathan, and Bryce went in his place. I don't know whether or not Imfeldt knew that Bryce was planning to murder Nathan. But they both must have assumed that Nathan had possession of Tom's photos—they probably thought he was going to blackmail Imfeldt—and that the only way to get rid of the incriminating evidence was to get rid of him." There was an extended pause. "I'm sorry."

*****

Aunt Sally and Arnold were waiting for me in the driveway when Dinah dropped me off. "Oh Lord, please," I muttered under my breath. "I really can't do this now."

I gave Dinah a hug and got out of the car. I could see that Aunt Sally was turned away from me, and as I made a fast beeline for the front door, I tried to make myself invisible by stooping to blend in with the brittlebush plants that lined our driveway.

"Yoo-hoo! Amanda!"

I heard a car door slam, and a moment later Aunt Sally was standing behind me as I was inserting my key in the front door.

"Aunt Sally," I said. "I didn't see you there."

"We've been waiting a long time for you to come home. Terry said that you'd left the station hours ago."

"We?" I said, and strained my eyes to see who was sitting in Arnold's front passenger seat. All I could see through the shrubs was the shadow of what appeared to be a man. For all I knew, it could have been a department store dummy Aunt Sally had gotten hold of to fool the highway patrol into believing she could legally drive in the HOV lane. "We who?"

"Me and Ernie. I brought him over to meet you." She flashed her left hand, its third finger displaying a large diamond ring. "We're engaged!"

Chapter Twenty-Eight

"Aunt Sally, I wish you'd have given me some notice. This really isn't a good time...I'm trying to reach Jeff, and..." I stopped in midsentence when I saw that crooked smile evaporate and those beady little eyes, magnified threefold through gigantic, round lenses, blink back tears. For all her quirks and irritating ways, Aunt Sally was my dad's baby sister, and, whatever the circumstances, he'd want me to treat her with kindness. Besides, I still owed her big-time for nearly getting her killed in Imfeldt's mine.

"You know what?" I said. "Go ahead and bring Ernie around to the patio. I'll bring out some lemonade and cookies."

Aunt Sally's impish grin returned. "We're celebrating, Amanda. Champagne would be nice, but if you don't have any on hand, Ernie likes gin and tonics with a twist. I guess cookies go good with those, too."

"Okay, but give me ten minutes."

I dropped my purse onto the sofa and stopped to check our landline for messages from Jeff. Nothing. *Where is he?! Why isn't he answering his phone?! He always answers his phone*!!

I turned on the TV and flipped through all the local stations, expecting to see a news flash: a grim reporter standing in front of the smoking remains of Marty Palmer's plane at the foot of South Mountain. But there was only the standard Saturday afternoon fare: sitcom reruns, sports, and cooking shows. I clicked off the set and hurried into the kitchen, where I poured myself a large, cold glass of Chardonnay before I grabbed gin, tonic, and limes from the refrigerator. I threw some Oreos onto a plate and carried a tray out to the patio. In profile, Ernie looked vaguely familiar.

"There she is!" said Aunt Sally, and poked Ernie in the arm. "There's my Amanda!"

Ernie turned to face me head-on, and I nearly dropped the tray. "We've already had the pleasure of meeting…kind of." I smiled dryly and addressed Ernie as I set the tray on the table in front of him. "How's your prostate these days?"

"Huh?" said Aunt Sally with a frown.

Ernie growled his response. "My prostate's none of your danged business!"

"You thought it was a few weeks ago at the Fry's Little Clinic," I said.

Ernie scowled at Aunt Sally. "Your niece is as loony as you are." He grabbed a drink from the tray. "Humph! I'll bet this drink is 99% tonic and 1% cheap gin."

"Ernie!" scolded Aunt Sally.

I took a seat at the far end of the table and pressed my lips firmly to the rim of my wine glass, hoping to take some comfort from it like a one-year-old takes comfort from a pacifier. "Mr. Saunders, isn't it?" I had to practically choke up and cough out the next words. "I understand that congratulations are in order. Aunt Sally told me the good news."

"What good news? What in blazes are you talking about?!"

This was going to be a long afternoon. I framed my sentences as questions. "Uh…your engagement? Aunt Sally tells me that you're going to be married?"

He turned to Aunt Sally and howled, "Have you lost your mind, woman?!"

Aunt Sally held out her hand and waved her ringed finger, its diamond sparkling in the intense midday sun, in front of Ernie's face. "But Ernie, honey, you gave me this ring!"

Ernie scraped the chair away from the table and stood. "Not to keep! You were supposed to take it to Esther's cousin, the jeweler, to have it appraised. It's Norma's ring. Why in blazes would I give it to you?!" Ernie held his gnarled hand, palm up, to Aunt Sally. "Hand it over right now, or I'll call the Sun Lakes Posse and have you thrown in jail."

"Who's Norma?" I asked.

"His dead wife." The only other time I'd seen Aunt Sally cry was at my dad's funeral. She took off the ring and said, "Here's your lousy ring, you old fool!" With that, she tossed the ring into the center of the swimming pool. The sun glinted off the diamond in a brilliant flash before the ring hit the water with a tiny plop and disappeared from view.

Ernie glared at her, then kicked off his orthopedic sandals and rolled up his pant legs to the knees. "You'll pay for this, Sally Buhler!"

"It's Mueller, Sally Mueller, you shyster! I never want to see you again!"

"No problem there, you old battle-axe!" said Ernie as he slowly let himself down the ladder into the pool.

I heard the phone ringing in the living room. "Aunt Sally," I said, "you'd better come inside with me. That might be Jeff." I wasn't sure whose safety I feared for most: Aunt Sally's or Ernie Saunders'. I only knew that I couldn't leave the two together alone near a body of water that was deep enough to drown in.

"Well, I'm not leaving the drinks out here for that old galoot to guzzle down." She hurriedly placed the platter of Oreos and the drinks on the tray and called, "Have a crappy life, Ernie Saunders! By the way, your singing is bad enough to make a goldfish jump out of its bowl and drown itself!"

I was relieved to see Jeff's number in the window display. I could hear his voice, but it was muffled since he was whispering frantically into the phone. Something was definitely wrong.

"Jeff, what's the matter?! I can barely hear you! Are you all right?!"

"Mom, I don't—owe—you…"

"Can you speak up? You don't owe me…what?!"

His voice was louder, and this time the words were clear. "I don't know what to do."

"What happened?! Where are you?!"

"Mr. Palmer's office." There was a pause, then nothing.

"Jeff?! Are you still there?!"

"I just went to see if Mr. Palmer was coming back yet. See, I left my cell in the plane after my lesson and I stopped back here to see if he had it. The door was open, so I walked in. My phone was on his desk, but he wasn't here. But I found—"

The next thing I heard was the sound of the phone hitting a hard surface, and then a loud drone signaling that the call had ended. To my Cluster C ears, it was the shrill sound of an air-raid siren warning of imminent danger: an approaching tornado or a nuclear attack. I scrolled to the last incoming call, punched the key, and an out-of-service message flashed on the screen.

Next, I phoned Terry, but the call went directly to voice mail. I tried the station's reception desk. "They're all in a meeting right now, Mrs. Winters. But it should be over in just a few minutes. I'll have Mr. Winters call you as soon as he can."

"Tell him it's urgent, that I think Jeff may be in trouble, and that I'm on my way to Marty Palmer's office.

I phoned Staatz, but he must have been on another call. The phone rang and rang, with no option for voice mail.

I debated whether I should call 9-1-1, and realized I wouldn't know what to say. *Help me, please! I was just talking to my son on the phone when all of a sudden the connection was lost!*

I grabbed my purse from the sofa and went into the kitchen, where Aunt Sally was stuffing Oreos into her mouth and getting ready to wash them down with the gin and tonic mix that remained in the pitcher.

"I get hungry and thirsty when I'm stressed out," she said.

"Aunt Sally, put that pitcher down! You have to drive me to ASU Polytechnic right now! I think Jeff's in trouble!"

We glanced out the kitchen window and saw the top of Ernie's bald head bobbing around.

"Do you think he'll be all right?" I asked, as I pictured Detective Staatz stopping by and finding a dead body floating in our pool.

"He's too mean to die," said Aunt Sally, pulling her keys from her purse. "Now let's take Arnold for a ride and find Jeffy."

To my relief, Aunt Sally didn't ask too many questions. I told her only that Jeff had called from Marty Palmer's office and that the call had ended abruptly. "It's probably nothing to worry about," I said. "Detective Staatz just told me that he was close to making an arrest in both Tom and Nathan's murders."

"He is? Who?!"

"Steven Bryce."

"The cowboy we met out at the Imfeldt estate? If he's the culprit, then why are you so riled up about Jeffy being with this Palmer guy?"

"I don't know...Jeff sounded strange—frightened even, and he doesn't scare easily. He started to tell me that he'd found something in Palmer's office, and then he was cut off. I tried calling him back right away but couldn't reach him." I leaned forward in the seat as if to urge the car forward. "Can't Arnold go any faster?"

"Not without getting a ticket he can't."

It took us a good half hour to reach ASU Polytechnic, a sprawling desert-landscaped campus surrounded by a number of supersized parking lots. Jeff's orange RAV4 was easy to spot, and Aunt Sally parked in the space next to it. At least he must still be somewhere on campus.

"Aunt Sally, do you mind walking with me to the main building over there? I'll need to check in to find out where Palmer's office is."

"I could walk, but you'd probably make better time without me. I'll stay here with Arnold and keep my eyes peeled for Jeffy."

I slammed the door, ran across the main parking lot, and circled around a huge cactus garden to the main administration building. The desk was manned by one student worker, and there were four people, all of them students, in the line ahead of me. I bypassed them all and rushed up to the desk.

"Please. This is an emergency," I said. "I need to know how to get to Marty Palmer's office."

One of the students in line looked at me with concern. "Is something wrong, ma'am?"

"I'm not sure yet. Right now, I just really need to find Palmer."

"I'll show you where his office his." He walked me over to the front door. "See that building directly opposite this one? That's Wanner Hall. Mr. Palmer's office is in room 319, on the third floor."

"Thanks." I was already out of breath from my cross-campus sprint, and now another one lay before me. I'd really have to amp up my exercise routine and get into shape.

I waved to Aunt Sally as I ran past the main parking lot, but she was too far away to see me. By the time I reached the Wanner Hall lobby, I was huffing and puffing, but I didn't wait for the elevator. I took the stairs two at a time, using one hand on the railing to pull myself upward. My body felt as though it weighed three hundred pounds, and gravity was working against me. When I reached the third floor, I was sure that I was about to pass out; I took a few moments to slow my breathing before following the signs to room 319. The door was open a crack, so I gave it a push and stepped inside.

"Jeff? Mr. Palmer?"

The office was empty. I turned to leave, and then paused as my foot struck something that went skidding across the carpet: Jeff's cell phone, or at least what remained of it. It looked as though someone had stomped on it; a number of plastic shards lay scattered on the floor.

I emerged from the building to see Marty Palmer's Silverado making a beeline for the parking lot exit and half-ran, half-walked back to Arnold. At that point, I'd begun to hyperventilate. There was no paper bag handy, so I stuck my face inside the front of my shirt and breathed. I couldn't pass out—not now. I looked up again to see Palmer turn right out of the lot. Someone was in the truck's passenger seat. It was Jeff: I'd recognize the familiar shape of that head at any distance. Given the odd angle of his neck, he was either asleep or hurt. The rest of my trek back to Arnold happened in dreamlike slow motion. I reached the Cadillac and threw open the passenger door.

"Aunt Sally, follow that truck!" *Truck!* It dawned on me then. Palmer's truck was larger than Aaron Hunter's, but it was about the same color. Palmer could have been the driver of the truck that had tried to run me and Dinah off the road the other night. The realization pushed my sense of panic to the near-explosion level. "We have to hurry!"

But Aunt Sally wasn't there. The driver's seat was empty, and I'd been too hysterical to notice. The keys were in the ignition, so she couldn't have gone far. I got out of the car and did an anxious dance around it, looking in every direction for my absentee chauffeur. I spotted Aunt Sally's figure, even tinier than normal since she'd just come out of the administration building at the far end of the cactus garden. At her current rate of speed, she would reach Arnold too late. We'd never be able to catch up to Palmer, or even be able to calculate in which direction he'd gone. I didn't take time to think about it: I was going to have to get behind Arnold's wheel and drive. I waved to Aunt Sally, and she returned a cheery flutter with a handkerchief. Without another moment's hesitation, I got into the driver's seat, buckled up, and turned the key in the ignition. The sound and feel of the motor revving up had the peculiar effect of making me feel wonderfully independent and horribly nauseated at the same time. As I turned right onto Ulysses Avenue—the thought flashed in my mind that I was, indeed, on quite an odyssey here, so the name was appropriate—I tried to ignore the jumble of signs that intruded on my peripheral vision and the blur of traffic that was flowing like a fast-moving stream in the remote distance.

Palmer's car was in clear view on the road in front of me. I hoped he wasn't heading for the freeway. I soon realized that was something I didn't have to worry about: He drove only a few blocks before turning into another parking lot. I did have some major concerns, however, about the planes flying low overhead as they took off or landed. The roar of their engines caused Arnold's chassis to jerk and sway as though he were caught in the crest of a tidal wave. I gripped the wheel tightly and closed my eyes for a moment, then remembered how it wasn't a good idea to drive with your eyes closed. I followed Palmer past a sign that announced *Phoenix-Mesa Gateway Airport*.

Concentrating on the truck's rear bumper, on which a sticker proclaimed, *I'd rather be flying*, I continued to follow Palmer as he pulled into one of several parking spaces that fronted a cluster of hangars and small private planes.

The airport's passenger terminal lay quite a stretch to the northeast. When I realized that I wouldn't have to deal with commercial airport traffic, I exhaled loudly and used both hands to give Arnold's steering wheel a victory tap. So far, so good: I hadn't lost consciousness, or even thrown up yet.

Hopefully, the nerve-wracking experience I was subjecting myself to was all for naught. Hopefully, the scenario was an innocent one: Palmer and Jeff were simply on their way to the airport, where another, impromptu flying lesson would take place. I would consider this a character-building exercise…behavioral therapy without the bill. The thought was comforting until I remembered the smashed phone on the floor of the office and the strange way Jeff had been slumped over in the truck. Suddenly, Roy Staatz's assurances about Palmer's innocence were meaningless.

I pulled into a parking spot between a UPS truck and an Airstream camper. Palmer had gotten out of his pickup and was pulling Jeff, who appeared to be unconscious, from the passenger seat. I looked around for help, but the closest activity was two hangars away.

"Help!" I screamed, but the only person who heard me over the roar of the planes taking off and landing was Marty Palmer. His head jerked around, and his mouth opened in a grimace of surprise.

I clenched my fists and stomped toward him. "What are you doing?! What's wrong with Jeff?!"

A sourness rose in my throat, and the air around me sparked and churned: the aura of a panic attack that threatened to be a bad one. *Not now!* I had to stop Palmer and get Jeff away from him. My senses sharpened when I noticed Palmer's eyes narrow and his lips turn up at the corners as he directed his gaze at something or someone behind me.

The next thing I knew, I was waking up in an airplane, with Jeff's inert form stretched out on the seat in front of me, as we soared high above the mountaintops.

Chapter Twenty-Nine

I leaned over the seat and felt Jeff's throat for a pulse. The fact that there was one gave me renewed determination to meet the challenge of the present situation (which admittedly looked quite bleak) and get both of us out of it alive. I tried not to look out the windows at the diaphanous layers of clouds that were racing past, but focused instead on the face of my son. His breathing was regular, and color was starting to come back to his cheeks.

"Jeff…Jeff, wake up!"

He was sprawled across what I thought must be the copilot's seat, assuming that the chief pilot sat on the same side of the vehicle as the driver of a car. Crawling between the seats to the front, I knelt next to Jeff and patted his cheeks softly, quickly increasing the pressure to a soft slapping. I screamed as the plane started to pitch, the sound of the engine abruptly changing from a dull whirr to a whining drone.

Jeff stirred, and his eyes fluttered open. He licked his lips and said, "Mom? What happened? Where are we?"

"I think someone drugged us," I said. "And we're in an airplane…somewhere over the mountains."

Jeff sat up and looked around the cockpit. "Where's Palmer?"

"That's a good question…" I said, my voice accelerating to a level above the sound of the plane's engine. "There's no room to hide in this thing!" I craned my neck to study the plane's tiny interior. "He must have bailed out."

"Do you see any more parachutes?" asked Jeff hopefully. "There were at least a couple stowed in the back during my lesson."

"I don't see any!" I glanced at the instrument panel, which was less complicated than I'd expected. By less complicated, I mean that although there was an infinite number of dials and screens, there appeared to be very few objects that one could actually push, pull, twist, or turn, like switches or toggles. "Do you think you can land this plane?"

"I don't know." He studied the controls and said, "I only had the one lesson."

"What about that Xbox flight thing?" I said, remembering countless hours of watching Jeff from the kitchen as he engaged in dogfights and missile drops on the TV screen in the family room.

"You mean Tom Clancy's HAWX? It's a flight-simulator game, but the controls in this cockpit are pretty different from the game pad."

I leveled a gaze at him. "Jeff, we don't have a choice. Either you figure out a way to get us safely to the ground, or we're not going to make it."

He shook himself alert. "We have to switch places," he said, his voice determined. "Like right now…"

I made myself as tiny as possible so that Jeff could slide past me and into the pilot's seat. The plane's nose fell, and we were suddenly in a near-vertical position. I took a hard fall into the front console and used my right hand to stop my body from crashing through the front windshield. My hand bent backward much farther than it was meant to, and I cried out in pain.

"Mom! Are you okay?"

"I think I just broke my wrist."

"Hold on. I'm going to try and level the plane." Jeff used one hand to pull up on what looked like a small steering wheel that someone had taken a huge bite out of.

"Why is that steering wheel so little? How can it possibly change the direction of a whole airplane?"

"It's called a 'yoke.'"

"I don't care if you call it 'Mary Jo,' as long as you can use it to land this plane in one piece."

I swallowed back the nausea that now merged with my pain to top off the experience. Without one or the other, I might be able to think clearly and actually help Jeff save the both of us. Between the movement of the plane, the pain, and the nausea, however, I had to focus my mind fully on keeping my stomach down where it belonged. I thought of Terry. I wished I had my own cell phone. I wished I'd thought to pick up the pieces of Jeff's phone in Palmer's office: At least we might be able to put them back together and make a few good-bye calls.

Jeff glanced at me in alarm. "Mom, are you having a panic attack?"

"No, I'm not having a panic attack. You know that my panic attacks occur for no particular reason. And since this would be a really good reason to have a panic attack, I'm guessing that, no, I'm not having one."

"Oka-a-y, then." Jeff studied the sky ahead, then turned to look out the left window, and to the right. "I'm going to try and turn this plane around and head back to the airport."

"How do you know if you're in your lane?" I asked. "There aren't any lines."

"That's what the transponder screen is for, Mom. See that bright red dot? That's us. If you see a blip heading toward it, it means that there might be a plane headed our way. It also shows the altitude of the plane, so we know if we have to adjust ours to avoid a crash."

"A blip that 'might' be a plane? What else could the blip be?"

"I don't know. A drone, maybe, or a flock of birds."

I thought of US Airways Flight 1549 and the Canadian geese that caused its engines to lose power before Captain "Sully" Sullenberger had landed the plane in Hudson Bay, saving 155 people in the process. The only problem was, in southern Arizona, there was no Hudson Bay in which to do a splash landing. There were quite a few pools in Scottsdale that might be large enough for landing a small plane, but I didn't think Jeff, with his limited flight experience, had yet built up the confidence to try it.

Jeff pulled up on the left side of the yoke, and the plane veered left. After an initial jerk, the turn was completed smoothly.

"Okay, that's done," I said. "Now what?"

"Now I push the throttle, here, to reduce our power."

"Reduce our power? Are you sure that's a good idea?"

"Then I pull this knob, and hopefully the landing gear will come down."

"Hopefully?"

Jeff turned to me. "Mom, I got this. You'd better buckle up for the landing, though. It's going to be rough."

I tried to obey, but my right wrist wasn't cooperating. I lay the buckle across the front of my midsection and said, "Just keep your eyes on the road— on the sky—ahead. Whatever you do, stay clear of those mountains."

"See that white strip ahead? That must be the airport. Now I just have to pull back on the yoke to slow down and keep the nose of the plane up so that it doesn't touch the ground."

Suddenly, the white strip was big as life, right there in front of us, just a few feet beneath the plane. I wasn't sure if it was the strip behind Palmer's hangar, but I wasn't about to quibble at this point.

"Hold on, Mom!"

The front wheels of the plane struck the ground, and the plane bounced back into the air so that the top of my head hit the ceiling of the cockpit.

"Mom, I told you to buckle up!"

"I couldn't manage the buckle because of my wrist, and you had other things to worry about," I said, rubbing my head with my left hand. "I'm fine."

Jeff tried another landing, and this time the wheels of the plane stayed on the ground. I used imaginary brakes to assist him in getting the plane to slow down so that we wouldn't end up crashing through the gate separating us from the main terminal.

When the plane finally stopped in a jagged stream of fits and starts, I burst into tears.

"Mom, what are you crying for? I landed the plane...we made it."

"These are tears of joy." I beamed at him and covered his right hand with my left. "You're an awesome son, you know that? I can't believe you just did what you did."

"I guess that Xbox really paid off," he said. He started to open the cockpit door, but turned back and said, "I see Arnold parked out there, but no Aunt Sally. How did you get here?"

"I drove," I said, omitting the fact that I'd driven less than three blocks.

He grinned. "You're pretty awesome yourself."

The happiness of the moment ended abruptly when I remembered that Palmer had just attempted to send Jeff and me crashing to our deaths. "Jeff, when you called me from Palmer's office, you were about to tell me that you'd found something. What was it? What did you find?"

"Nate's laptop and phone. I didn't see Palmer, so I opened a door, thinking that maybe his office had more than one room, but it was a closet. Nate's stuff was just sitting out there in the open. And there were a few other things inside that closet—weird things—a pile of dirty old clothes, a long black wig, and a fake beard."

Chapter Thirty

"I didn't hear Palmer come into the office," Jeff continued. "Man, he was acting crazy. He grabbed my phone and trashed it. Then he went over to the closet door and slammed it shut. He made up some lame excuse about Nate giving Danielle his laptop and phone to hold onto that night—the night he was killed—because they were going to a movie later and Nate didn't want to take his stuff."

"And the wig and the beard?"

"Palmer said they were left over from the faculty Halloween party. I told him that he needed to turn over Nate's stuff to Detective Staatz right away, and that if he didn't, I would."

"And then what did he say?"

"He told me to go ahead and take Nate's stuff. But when I opened the closet door, he shoved me from behind and locked me in. He came back later with some other guy I've never seen before. He came at me with a syringe. And then I woke up here on this plane with you slapping me in the face."

"We have to get to a phone and call 9-1-1," I said. I used my good hand to open the door on my side of the plane and was about to climb out when I noticed there was a three-foot drop to the ground. "I'm going to need some help to get down from here."

"Wait for me to come around," said Jeff, as he climbed out through the pilot-side door. I turned to watch him disappear behind the plane's tail. A few seconds later, my door was pulled open wide, but it wasn't Jeff who was standing on the ground below.

"Mrs. Winters." Marty Palmer reached his arm up toward me. "Let me give you a hand."

"You can give me a hand by getting out of my way."

Jeff reappeared next to Palmer. His arms were securely held behind his back by Steven Bryce.

Bryce's grin stretched ear-to-ear. "Marty, looks like you have some competition. The kid was able to land this here plane without a scratch."

"So you're the coward who came up behind me with a needle," I said to Bryce. "And I suppose you picked up your friend, here, from wherever the wind blew his parachute."

Palmer cocked his head toward the nearest hangar. "Let's continue this discussion inside, shall we? It's too noisy out here, what with the roar of the planes and all."

I shook his hand off my arm and winced in pain. "We're not going anywhere with you. Jeff, stay right where you are."

Palmer and Bryce drew handguns from their pockets, and there was a loud click in stereo as they simultaneously cocked the triggers. "Ma'am, I suggest you and your son move on into the hanger, now," said Bryce in his sickening drawl.

Jeff looked at me, the expression on his face reflecting fear and confusion. I nodded reluctantly, and he allowed Bryce to nudge him along toward the hangar. As Palmer used his gun to urge me forward, I studied the area around us. A small plane had just landed at a nearby runway, but it was still taxiing when we disappeared into the hangar. It was unlikely that the pilot had even noticed us.

Two small planes were parked inside the hangar. It was a beautiful day...maybe one of the planes' owners would decide to take a little hop to Sedona or Flagstaff. He or she would walk in at any moment and see that we were in trouble. They'd call 9-1-1, and—

Jeff spun and knocked Bryce's gun out of his hand, and Palmer aimed his gun squarely at Jeff's head. Keeping my right arm flat against my side, I tackled Palmer by jamming hard into him from the left. "Jeff, run!"

Jeff nearly made it. He would have, too, if Bryce hadn't immediately reclaimed his gun and got off a shot. The bullet hit Jeff in the shoulder, and he dropped heavily to the ground. Blood instantly began to pool on the concrete floor beneath him. Knowing that the next bullet would be meant for me but not caring at this point, I ran to Jeff and knelt beside his prone body. Blood was running from his wound much too fast. I tore one of the sleeves from my shirt, wrapped Jeff's arm tightly, and whispered a prayer. The bleeding slowed and seconds later came to a full stop. I looked over at Bryce and Palmer, who were just standing there, watching me with amusement.

"I guess one more murder at this point doesn't matter to you guys, huh?" My voice was hoarse with emotion. "First you killed Tom Reynolds, then his son, and then, I suspect, Dieter Imfeldt. I have to assume you're trying for a full house, here."

Palmer stepped forward and said, "Tom Reynolds was Imfeldt's idea. If I hadn't done it, he would have found someone else to do it for him."

"What about Nathan? Why him?"

Bryce, his gun pointed at my face, walked up to me. "Marty, why are we wastin' time chattin' it up with this busybody? Let's get rid of her and the kid right now. We can stow their corpses in the cargo hold and dump them in the desert come nightfall."

Suddenly the air around me began to spin. I was beginning to understand that maybe my panic attacks did happen for a valid reason every now and then. I swallowed bile and focused on Jeff. He was still conscious, but the color of his face told me that he was clearly on the edge of passing out.

Palmer seemed to be the more amiable of the two, so I concentrated on him. "I was Nathan's godmother. I deserve to know why he died. You owe me that much."

"Imfeldt got a call from Nathan," said Palmer, "saying that he'd found some papers that belonged to his dad. Naturally, Imfeldt got nervous about it. He went to Bryce, here, for some advice. He said he wanted to meet with the boy. He thought Nathan had found whatever evidence Tom had against him and was going to blackmail him with it. Bryce filled me in, and I offered to stand in for Imfeldt at the meeting with Nathan."

I nodded. "That's pretty much the conclusion I came to. The wig, the beard, and the old clothes Jeff found in your office closet. That's what you wore when you met with Nathan. You didn't want him to recognize you."

Palmer smiled. "Like I told you at the funeral, I'd never met Nathan. But I didn't want any of my students to spot me in the area. Mill Avenue on a Friday night is flooded with college kids. I couldn't take the chance one of them would see me."

"Why didn't you just throw Nathan's laptop and phone into the river when you shot him? Why hang onto them?"

"I didn't know what the kid had on them, so I couldn't leave them behind."

"And planting the bike in Anthony Hunter's yard…whose idea was that?"

"That was rich, wasn't it? Stevie came up with that one. We had to get rid of it, so what better place to do it than on the old Indian's property? It was kind of like getting back at him for all the trouble he stirred up for us ten years ago."

I knew that the longer I kept them talking, the greater the chance someone would walk in on us. I kept going. "What about Dieter Imfeldt? His death wasn't a suicide, was it?"

Palmer smiled and shook his gun toward Bryce. "Steve, you can take it from here."

Bryce glared at him, but when Palmer shrugged and waved him on with the gun, he spoke up. "Like Marty said, when Imfeldt heard about the Reynolds kid's murder, danged if he didn't get all jumpy. He said that he was going to the police. He was going to confess everything."

"Everything, meaning bringing DDT across the border illegally," I said. I looked at Palmer. "Which I suspect your pilot friend, here, flew in from Mexico…from Matesa Industriales, to be specific."

Bryce, being careful to keep the gun level and aimed at me, half-folded his arms in a pose of confidence. "Well, now, I'm just impressed with your understanding of the entire situation, ma'am. I didn't give a rat's behind if Imfeldt wanted to confess to the DDT thing. I did, however, mind the fact that he wanted to fess up to Tom Reynold's murder. I mean, Marty, here, did the actual dirty work, but I was there in that mine watchin' the whole thing go down. And there were witnesses…not witnesses to the act itself, of course—Marty and I are too smart for that—but witnesses who would have been able to place both of us at the scene." He saw the expression on my face and added, "Aw, don't go feelin' too bad about the old man…he was goin' to die soon anyway."

Palmer added, "You might even say we did him a favor…put him out of his misery."

My heart started to pound in my chest, and my body suddenly felt as though it were beginning to melt into the concrete floor. I fell to the ground and began to retch. I was dry-heaving at this point, but I knew what was about to follow.

"What's wrong with you?!" Palmer yelled. Scowling, he stood over me, then reached down and pulled me up roughly by the arm.

"Ow! My wrist!" I cried. Because, of course, my wrist was broken, and my arm was connected to it.

I opened my mouth to warn Palmer, but what spewed out was a stream of vomit that soaked his arm and the front of his shirt. He jumped back in disgust, and I could tell that his grip on the gun weakened as he hoisted both hands into the air. I felt better, my stomach now empty, and something inside me sparked to life. With my good left hand, I grabbed the gun from Palmer and waved it back and forth between him and Bryce.

"Bryce, drop your gun or your partner, here, is a dead man." I hoped I sounded sincere, and I also hoped I sounded like someone who knew how to use a gun.

Bryce laughed. "Go ahead and shoot him. It makes no never-mind to me."

"Well, let me explain what's going to happen now," I said. "Bryce, you're going to drop that gun. Then you and Palmer are going to put your hands in the air where I can see them, and you're going to walk out of this building. I'll be right behind you. We're heading over to the main terminal, and we're not stopping before we get there unless we happen to come across someone with a phone."

"You still look a little green around the gills," Palmer said as he stripped down to his T-shirt and rolled his soiled shirt into a ball before throwing it aside in disgust. "Are you sure you know how to shoot that thing?"

"I really don't think you want to find out."

"You know, you made your first mistake by snooping around that mine," said Palmer. "You should have left well enough alone." He glanced over at Jeff, who had managed to pull himself to the wall and into a half-sitting position. "If you had, your son, over there, wouldn't be bleeding to death right now."

I'm ashamed to say I fell for it: I turned to look at Jeff, which took my focus off Bryce and Palmer long enough for Palmer to once again grab the gun from my hand.

"Bryce, you take the kid back to the plane, and I'll make sure that Mommy Dearest, here, doesn't try any more stupid tricks." He dug the muzzle of the gun deep into my back. The pain had one benefit in that it took my mind off the throbbing of my wrist. "We're going for another little airplane ride, only this time Steve and I will be right there with you."

"Where are we going?" I asked, dreading the answer.

Palmer broke into a wide grin. "I know a beautiful spot in the desert…somewhere nice and private."

I watched from behind as Bryce half-pushed, half-dragged Jeff toward the plane. I looked around frantically for someone I could cry out to for help, but the nearest person was a good distance from the hangar and walking away from us toward the main terminal. Jeff and I were unceremoniously thrown into the back of the cockpit of Palmer's plane. My wrist made a cracking sound when I landed on it, and I bit my lip and forced back the tears. I didn't want these murderers to see me cower. I adjusted Jeff's position so that he wasn't lying on his wounded shoulder, and noticed that the bleeding had started to ooze again. He seemed to be drifting away, and his face was now drained of all color. Palmer had already started the plane and was taxiing for the lift-off. I had to do something, and I had to do it fast: I was now in so much pain that, panic attack or no panic attack, losing consciousness threatened to be only seconds away.

I screamed, louder than I'd ever screamed before. I screamed louder than a banshee, louder than a pack of wolves howling at the moon, louder, even, than my dad's demonic smoke alarm. Even I had to cringe at the sheer magnitude of the howling that filled the plane's tiny cabin, which I'd turned into an echo chamber of horrors. I leaned forward and wrapped my left arm around Palmer's throat. I don't know where my strength came from. It must have been pure adrenaline. If I could have used my right hand, I would have dug my fingers into his eyes. Instead, I pulled back and down on his head, pressing it into the seat. I held fast to him while my torso and head bobbed and weaved up and down, back and forth, all the while not letting up on my screaming. Bryce, eyes wide and mouth agape, sat by helplessly. He couldn't risk shooting off his gun inside the cockpit: If he missed me, the bullet might carom and bounce back to hit him or Palmer. Palmer lost his grip on the yoke, and even if he hadn't, he wouldn't be able to see where he was going because of the angle of his head. The plane veered off-course and started to roll toward the steel mesh fence that separated the runway from the road.

I stopped screaming only when my vision caught the flashing lights of a fast-moving stream of police vehicles just a few blocks away on Ulysses Avenue and headed toward the airport. "Turn off the engine!" I ordered Bryce, not relinquishing my hold on Palmer. "This plane isn't going anywhere."

Epilogue

What follows is a recap of the events that preceded and followed the arrests of Marty Palmer and Steven Bryce.

After the station's receptionist gave Terry my message, he'd called Staatz to let him know that I thought Jeff might be in trouble and that I was on my way to Palmer's office. In the university parking lot, Staatz encountered a very angry Aunt Sally, who'd gone to the administration building in search of a bathroom (thanks to the three gin and tonics she'd managed to put away before Ernie's meltdown). She'd told Staatz I'd absconded with Arnold and had taken off toward the airport.

Earlier, Staatz had confronted Anita Reyes at Matesa Industriales and convinced her to give up the names of the men (Palmer and Bryce), who, ten years before, had actually completed the illegal purchase and transport of the DDT on behalf of Dieter Imfeldt. It seems that Staatz had been able to leverage the fact that Ms. Reyes had some family members who'd been living in Phoenix without the benefit of green cards. Staatz also figured I must have had a good reason for ignoring my driving phobia to chase after Palmer and called in the Mesa PD. Everyone converged on the scene and apprehended Palmer and Bryce, who, after my ear-shattering (and quite effective, I might add) assault, seemed eager to reach the relative tranquility of the backseat of a squad car.

Jeff and I were both taken by ambulance to the hospital, where he underwent surgery for his gunshot wound and was released shortly thereafter to recover at home with Terry and me. I, on the other hand, needed only a wrist splint and some strong meds.

Marty Palmer and Steven Bryce have since been charged with three counts of first-degree murder, which should get them, at minimum, life sentences. Bryce was also charged with two counts of attempted murder after he confessed to using Imfeldt's Caterpillar to block the mine entrance, and two additional counts after syringes containing ketamine, the knockout drug he'd used on me and Jeff, were found in his jacket pocket. He also confessed to breaking into Dinah's garage and trashing Jeff's apartment (though he couldn't be charged for the latter since the door hadn't been locked). This is Arizona, so there's always the possibility that both sentences might take a turn and land the murderers in a place far worse—and much hotter—than a stuffy jail cell in a state prison.

Dinah has gone back to work in an attempt to lose herself in the world of open houses and short sales. She continues to attend meetings with her grief support group and plans to volunteer for the New Song Center for Grieving Children, an organization that assists children who have lost a parent. She's also in the process of starting an ASU scholarship fund in Nathan's name.

Aaron and Anthony Hunter were extremely grateful to have their names fully cleared. Aaron is lead singer for a rock band that he recently put together and which plays Friday nights at the Cottonwood Club. Anthony still enjoys his Friday night poker games, and he's invited Terry to sit in whenever he can.

Aunt Sally insists that she's done with men. Terry and I have placed bets on how long that will last.

Detective Staatz announced that he'll be moving to the Maricopa County Sheriff's Department, District 1, which encompasses both Ocotillo Springs and Sun Lakes. He told Dinah that he made the move so that he could keep a "close eye" on her. I'm pretty sure he meant that literally.

I'm now driving a little—short trips to the supermarket, the library, and church, all of which are within a few blocks of our home. I've undergone a bit of a transformation during the past month, which has prompted me to enjoy a newfound confidence approaching independence. I'm guessing this is how normal, non-Cluster C adults must feel most of the time. Former Detective (now Deputy Commander) Roy Staatz has submitted an official request for me to work as a consultant for his district. He said he was impressed with my critical-thinking and problem-solving abilities, so I highlighted those on my resume. We'll see what happens.

Spring has returned to southeast Arizona in glorious color: The cactus wrens are nesting, the desert is blooming, and there's the promise that normalcy, goodness, and most important…laughter…will once more prevail in the Valley.

THE END

ABOUT THE AUTHOR

 Carmen Will is a freelance writer and editor whose novel, *A Practicum for Murder*, was a finalist in Poisoned Pen Press' 2013 Discover Mystery contest. In April 2015, Will's short story, *Please Don't Pick the Lemons,* was featured on *Mash Stories*, a website that promotes fiction writing and publishes selected short stories.

Will, who earned a B.A. in Professional Communication with a specialization in writing and editing, lives in Sun Lakes, Arizona with her husband Wayne and is currently working on her second Amanda Winters mystery.

www.ingramcontent.com/pod-product-compliance
Lightning Source LLC
Chambersburg PA
CBHW050417260626
47156CB00003B/1053